BIRDS
WITHOUT
A NEST

TEXAS
PAN AMERICAN
SERIES

BIRDS WITHOUT A NEST A NOVEL

by CLORINDA MATTO DE TURNER

Translation by
J. G. H. (1904)

Emended by
Naomi Lindstrom (1996)

*A Story of Indian Life
and Priestly Oppression
in Peru*

 UNIVERSITY OF TEXAS PRESS
AUSTIN

Emendation of the English translation of Clorinda Matto de Turner's 1889 *Aves sin nido* by J. G. H. published in 1904 by Charles J. Thynne, London, under the title *Birds without a Nest: A Story of Indian Life and Priestly Oppression in Peru*. Every effort has been made to trace any copyright owners. The University of Texas Press will be happy to hear from any who proved impossible to contact.

Requests for permission to reproduce material from this work should be sent to Permissions, University of Texas Press, Box 7819, Austin, TX 78713-7819.

LIBRARY OF CONGRESS CATALOGING-IN-PUBLICATION DATA

Matto de Turner, Clorinda, 1852–1909
  [Aves sin nido. English]
  Birds without a nest : a novel / by Clorinda Matto de Turner; translation by J.G.H. (1904); emended by Naomi Lindstrom (1996).
      p.   cm. — (Texas Pan American series)
  "A story of Indian life and priestly oppression in Peru." Introd. includes bibliographical references.
      ISBN 0-292-75194-X (cloth : alk. paper). — ISBN 0-292-75195-8 (paper : alk. paper)
      I. J.G.H. II. Lindstrom, Naomi, 1950– . III. Title. IV. Series.
PQ8497.M3A913   1996
863—DC20   95-44768

Contents

Foreword   vii
Author's Preface   1

PART ONE

1   The Town of Killac   5
2   The Yupanqui Family   6
3   Indian Loans, 500 Per Cent   10
4   White House   11
5   Priest and Governor   12
6   Juan's Return Home   17
7   Fernando's Gift to Lucia   19
8   Danger Ahead   21
9   A Stratagem   25
10   Rosalia Restored   28
11   Doña Petronila   31
12   Marcela Pays the Preist   32
13   Sold to Rochino   34
14   The Plot   37
15   The Assault   42
16   Hope Renewed   46
17   Evil Deeds   48
18   The Indian's Gratefulness   50
19   Melitona Gleaning News   52
20   The Burial of Juan   56
21   Manuel and His Mother   59
22   The Instigators Interviewed   62
23   A Secret Revealed   66
24   A Shot That Missed Its Mark   70

25 Marcela Follows Juan 72
26 The Priest's Confession 74
27 Sebastian's Bad Conscience 76

PART TWO

28 Fernando and the Judge 79
29 Manuel, a Good Teacher 82
30 Colonel Paredes 85
31 Tired of Killac 88
32 No Need of a Warrant 91
33 The Wrong One Imprisoned 96
34 Going to Lima 98
35 Father Pascual's Solitude 101
36 Talking It Over 106
37 Fleecing the Indian 109
38 Margarita and Manuel 111
39 Doubts, Fears, and Hopes 116
40 Teodora's Escape 118
41 The Pursuit 121
42 Manuel's Birth Veiled 124
43 The Hide, Then the Flesh 129
44 A Heroine of Love 132
45 One Against Five Thousand 135
46 Fernando Enlightens Lucia 137
47 Martina Visits Isidro 142
48 Fernando's Proposal 144
49 The Departure and Arrest 147
50 Comments 152
51 To the Station 154
52 Manuel Follows 157
53 The Journey by Rail 160
54 The Prisoners Released 163
55 A Terrible Shock 167
56 Grand Imperial Hotel 170
57 The Agate Cross 173
58 Birds without a Nest 178

FOREWORD Clorinda Matto de Turner
(1852–1909; born Grimanesa
Martina Matto Usandivares in El Cuzco, Peru) is today remembered for her 1889 *Aves sin nido* (*Birds without a Nest: A Story of Indian
Life and Priestly Oppression in Peru*, 1904). This novel, which ignited
fiery controversy upon its appearance, declined in reputation
during the early twentieth century. However, the novel and its
author have in subsequent years earned the appreciation of new
audiences. The recent wave of readers shows a greater awareness
of Matto's perspective as a woman intellectual in nineteenth-
century Peru. New recognition has gone to the feminism that, together with the more obvious protest against the exploitation of
Indians and clerical corruption, runs through *Birds without a Nest*.

Most of the novel's readers today are attracted by the information and insights it provides concerning race, ethnicity, gen-
der, and nineteenth-century progressive thought. *Birds without a
Nest* exercises an appeal similar to that of the fiction of Rosario
Castellanos (Mexico, 1925–1974). Both writers are able to reveal
simultaneously the relations between Indians and non-Indians
and those between women and men, and both bring to their
work an unusually close acquaintance with a living indigenous
culture. *Birds without a Nest* is valued and discussed above all as a
source of historical and cultural knowledge, the focus of the
present foreword. Its novelistic construction has frequently been
singled out for its flaws, while only the most negative critic would
deny the social and historical significance of *Birds without a Nest*
and its value for students of progressive thought concerning native peoples and women. Luis Mario Schneider summarizes the
general judgment: "*Birds without a Nest* is a work of greater socio-
logical than artistic interest." [1]

Yet its form and style are complex enough to sustain critical discussion. One of the most original and careful studies of *Birds without a Nest*, by John S. Brushwood, concerns the work's structure. Analyzing the novel's imagery, its narrator, and other features, Brushwood shows the central opposition around which Matto has constructed her best-known work.[2] Though Brushwood is more appreciative of the novel's design than are most critics, he does not argue that Matto exhibited outstanding skill in the organization of her text. Rather, "Clorinda Matto was very aware of the act of making a novel," and *Aves sin nido* reveals a conscious, efficacious struggle to use the novelist's craft for social ends.[3]

There is some dispute whether *Birds without a Nest* is the first Spanish American novel in the *indigenista* subgenre, focusing upon contemporary Indian characters and emphasizing the native community's plight. In the general perception, Matto de Turner's novel stands out as the first *indigenista* novel. Schneider, noting how common this belief is, reminds readers of earlier Peruvian examples, one nearly contemporary and one from 1848.[4] Nonetheless, he argues that *Birds without a Nest* is "the first novel in which the Indian is no longer simply used for esthetic purposes and emerges as a social entity, showing the situation of the Indian dominated and exploited by political and clerical power."[5]

It is certainly the first Spanish American novel to electrify a wide audience with episodes in which governmental and clerical authorities take advantage of the native population. While many readers found *Birds without a Nest* scandalous, it met with acclaim from progressives. In February of 1890, the then-president of Peru, Andrés Avelino Cáceres, wrote Matto a lengthy letter praising *Birds without a Nest* for its accurate and knowledgeable depiction of social conditions in the sierra of the Andes; he said that the novel had stimulated him in his pursuit of needed reforms.

Birds without a Nest drew fire as well as praise. The Catholic Church, whose small-town parish priests had been characterized as lecherous and corrupt, saw in Matto a dangerous detractor. In 1890, the year after *Birds without a Nest* appeared, Matto gave the church an opening to retaliate. She was editor of *El Perú*

Ilustrado, Lima's most noted literary review, when it published a short story by Henrique Maximiano Coelho Neto in which Christ was shown as sexually drawn to Mary Magdalene. Not only *El Perú Ilustrado* but Matto's novel were singled out as defamatory to the church. A controversy broke out, involving a good many of Peru's intellectuals. Before it ended, Matto was excommunicated, forced to resign her editorship, and burned in effigy in El Cuzco and Arequipa; her novel was placed on the Index of Prohibited Books.

Of the novel's several themes, the most evident are its protest over the treatment of the Andean Indians and its criticism of clerical, judicial, and governmental authorities in small towns. Matto's social vision had been formed in great part by the teachings of Manuel González Prada (1848–1918); she and he were both important figures in the progressive intellectual circles of Lima. *Aves sin nido* is dedicated to this mentor. González Prada was the thinker who, in an influential formulation, characterized the sources of the Indians' oppression as a triad consisting of the judge, the (town) governor, and the priest.[6] Matto states overtly in her preface to the novel that these small-town authorities, wielding the power they do, must be more carefully selected and monitored. In the course of *Birds without a Nest*, these three types of authorities are repeatedly identified as the sources of corruption and abuse.

Though the novel does not completely specify the measures needed to improve the condition of Peru's Indians, it offers a number of recommendations. Clearly, Matto is trying to bring about not a revolution or restructuring of society but rather reforms within the existing system. These include better schooling and nutrition for Indians, educating non-Indians about the indigenous peoples' situation and culture, and closer oversight of local officials. The novel also advocates the abolition of such abuses as forcing Indians into domestic service and maintaining them in a hopeless state of debt.

One of the novel's characters, the progressive mining administrator Fernando, says that "all Peruvians" must find answers to the plight of native communities. Yet *Birds without a Nest* makes its plea to certain Peruvians, non-Indian progressives who are in a position to pressure the government and church for reform. In the twentieth century, some readers have faulted Matto's novel for assigning the responsibility for change so heavily to non-Indian reformers. Later approaches to problems facing native communities would envision Indians as more active agents of change. In addition, *Birds without a Nest* prescribes a specific remedy for clerical lechery. Matto asserts in her preface and demonstrates throughout her novel "the need for a married clergy as a social necessity."

The portraits of native characters constitute one of the great innovations of *Birds without a Nest*. Of course, the novel is designed to illustrate concepts and, as a result, allows for little ambiguity and subtlety in the depiction of any of its characters. Even given this inherent limitation, the Indian protagonists, and above all two Indian wives and mothers, are differentiated and individualized to a degree previously unknown in the literary treatment of native characters. Matto was clearly seeking to win readers over to the pro-Indian cause with memorable and engaging indigenous characters rather than an oppressed mass. Marcela Yupanqui and Martina Champi stand out for their determination, resourcefulness, and spirited response to crises. Marcela's husband Juan reacts to the same situations with depression and despair. Marcela's daughter Margarita is distinguished by her "singular beauty" and ability to win the heart. Isidro Champi, sexton, bell ringer, and owner of livestock, and his wife Martina are distinguished by an economic and social position above that of the other Indians. However bold, clever, or economically advantaged the Indians may be, though, they are powerless to deal with the authorities.

The non-Indian characters are divided between enlightened progressives, who seek to improve the situation of beleaguered local Indians, and figures of backwardness and exploitation. Many of the good characters have been educated in Lima, seen as the center of enlightened thought; yet one, the boundlessly good-hearted Petronila, embodies an inborn, untutored sense of social justice.

Though they are passionate in their efforts to rescue persecuted and abused Indians, these progressives occasionally exhibit a sober awareness that campaigns on behalf of individuals can never solve the more general problems confronting the native population. As Fernando reflects after learning of a successful struggle to exonerate an unjustly imprisoned Indian, "So you have freed Isidro Champi. Oh! Who will free his entire disinherited race?" To this question, the idealistic young law student Manuel replies, "That is a question that should be asked of all Peruvians, my dear friend . . . !"

Matto's treatment of the situation of Peru's native population continued to attract controversy over the years. José Carlos Mariátegui (1894–1930), best known for his 1928 *Siete ensayos de interpretación de la realidad peruana* (*Seven Interpretive Essays on Peruvian Reality*, 1971), had a conflict-filled relation with Matto and her celebrated novel. Mariátegui, though of a younger generation than Matto, was also one of the intellectual heirs of Manuel González Prada. While Matto favored educational and reform measures, Mariátegui laid the conceptual outlines for an Andean socialism. Although his *Seven Essays* includes a discussion of the present state and future of literature on Indian themes, Mariátegui makes no mention of *Birds without a Nest*, at that time the best-known Peruvian work about Indians. His reasons for omitting *Birds without a Nest* are not difficult to guess. Matto undisguisedly sought to instill a desire for reform among educated, non-Indian readers. Mariátegui, while obviously also writing for white progressives, advocated a socialist reorganization of Peruvian society. As much of the conceptual underpinning as possible would originate in indigenous social thought, with its strong communitarian emphasis. Though a critic today could scarcely attempt to deny Matto's novel its historical importance and widespread impact, some observers share Mariátegui's uneasiness over its insistence that reforms are the answer. Antonio Cornejo Polar, perhaps the current-day critic best versed in Matto's work, typifies this objection: "Reading *Birds without a Nest*, one may receive at times the impression that the problems of those who oppress remote towns and the atrocious situation of the Indians could be solved if the town governor, the judge, and the priest would just carry out their obligations." [7]

Mariátegui's deliberate omission of Matto most likely depressed the novel's critical reputation for years. Critics often viewed it as more efficacious advocacy than literature, though it continued to be a popular novel that was regularly reissued. In 1934, Concha Meléndez, in her study of Spanish American novels on Indian themes, gave *Birds without a Nest* a thoughtful and sympathetic treatment, pointing out how great a step forward it had been in the literary depiction of Indians.[8] Meléndez, who was especially concerned with the situation of women intellectuals, caused an upturn in the critical reputation of *Birds without a Nest*.

Birds without a Nest is also a feminist novel. Readers have often been struck by the many reflections voiced by both the narrator and the characters concerning the inherent capabilities of women and society's lack of appreciation for them. To understand the novel's feminism, it is necessary to take into account that the feminism of a nineteenth-century Peruvian novel will not correspond in all respects to the international feminism of the late twentieth century.

Birds without a Nest is undeniably favorable to women. While the novel contains several male villains, the women characters are all good. In Matto's novelistic vision, women are more governed by ethics than are men. When Fernando observes that in Peru's small towns "women and men are nothing alike in their behaviour," his wife Lucia adds, "If the women were bad, too, this would be a hell!" Petronila illustrates Matto's concept that women exercise a morally corrective influence upon men, if the latter will only respect their judgment. Petronila is repeatedly seen prodding her vacillating husband, the town governor, to turn away from the corruption and violence toward which he can easily be drawn. Three male characters, Fernando, Manuel, and Gaspar, express the belief that women are quicker-witted than men and possess exceptional talents for guessing others' thoughts and actions. Fernando summarizes the concept: "Women always excel us in insight and imagination." The narrator on several occasions suggests that women are insufficiently valued by both individual men and society in general and that men should express appreciation for women's talents.

Birds without a Nest can easily appear inconsistent in the statements it makes about women's role. Cornejo Polar has complained of its "vague, romantic feminism."[9] Cornejo is disturbed by the novel's sentimental idealization of the angelic wife and mother and the innocent maiden. No doubt many readers have received a shock upon discovering that the novel's only overt allusion to the feminist movement is a disparaging one. The narrator describes the refined heroine Lucia as "leaving to [her husband] the business and turmoil of life and following out the grand ideas of the Spanish writer, which she had read many times, seated at her mother's side: 'Forget, poor women, your dreams of emancipation and liberty. Those are theories of sickly minds which can never be practised, because woman was born to grace the home.'"

At the core of the confusion is the degree of independence women should ideally attain. The narrator rejects those "dreams of emancipation and liberty" that could lead women to neglect the home. Yet the novel subjects to mockery antifeminist rhetoric that is based on a lack of respect for women. The novel's villainous characters denigrate initiatives coming from women. Petronila's husband tries to reject her good moral advice by saying, "Really, women should never mix themselves up with men's business; they had better keep to their pots and pans." Fernando stands out for his appreciation of his wife Lucia's quick thinking and moral steadfastness. At one point, he is musing inwardly, admiring his wife's exceptional seriousness of purpose. This passage concludes with the narrator's reflection, appearing to mirror Fernando's thoughts: "The Peruvian woman is docile and virtuous as a general rule." The choice of *docile* is especially surprising since Fernando has just observed Lucia taking some independent action whose purpose she does not disclose to him.

These contradictions and other similar ones can be explained to some degree as typical of much nineteenth-century feminism in its efforts to win wider social acceptance. This early feminism created the ideal of women who could act with considerable independence, yet still be first and foremost wives and, especially, mothers. Moderate feminists often justified proposed reforms by arguing that educated women, enjoying a respected status in society, would be better wives and mothers; mothers are often viewed as teachers who must prepare to give lessons. *Birds without a Nest* follows this tendency. It extols, throughout, the ideals of marriage and family life for all. Its good characters all appear in the context of a close family, and the narrator several times points to failure to marry and disrespectful husbands as scourges of society. Stronger education and greater respect for women are depicted as means of strengthening motherhood and the family, which in turn are seen as means of education. For example, when Lucia asks Fernando about the future of the Indian orphans who have joined their household, he responds that the couple must make plans to educate them. He explains his choice by saying, "We will place them in the college best adapted to form wives and mothers."

Cornejo Polar, considering the passages of seemingly antifeminist rhetoric, notes that they are not consistent with the action of the novel. The female characters by no means limit themselves to tending the hearth: "The women of *Aves sin nido* do enter determinedly into 'the business and turmoil of life' (like Doña Lucia summoning to her house the town's notable citizens to demand that they stop exploiting Yupanqui or like Doña Petronila defending the Marins' house when it is attacked by a mob, and they do so with the evident blessing of the narrator, the same narrator who assigns woman the exclusive function of 'gracing the home.'" [10] Cornejo attributes the idealization of the woman in the home, which he finds anachronistic for the late 1880s, to the novel's persistent romanticism.[11]

Matto's real-world statements and behavior yield the same picture of her feminism. In her twenties, she earned considerable popularity and esteem as a writer. While Matto wrote in many styles and genres, she earned her success with a type of local-color sketches, called *tradiciones*, invented and popularized by Ricardo Palma (1833–1919); she won the public approbation of the creator of the genre. She became a celebrated figure, appearing at the events of the literary world, joining Lima's most influential intellectual circles, and organizing her own salon. She earned her own living following the 1881 death of her husband, the Englishman Joseph Turner. As Mary G. Berg observes, in 1883 Matto became "the first woman in America to lead an important newspaper" (*La Bolsa* [Market News] in Arequipa, Peru).[12] In Lima she founded a press, Imprenta La Equitativa (The Equitable Press), staffed entirely by women. She advocated strengthening girls' and women's education. On the basis of Matto's career, the activities she promoted, and her writings, Berg and other critics have considered her an outstanding nineteenth-century feminist.[13]

Yet in Matto's public statements and essays, just as in her best-known novel, she drew the line at any form of feminism that would deflect woman from "that mission that God has assigned to her . . . by choosing her for motherhood."[14] In the preface to her 1886 literary textbook for girls and women, Matto again recommends for women only those forms of independence that pose no threat to motherhood, which she sees as a teaching career: woman "is not called to the pulpit, nor to the turbulence of public affairs, but to the teaching of her family, to the peace of the home and the gracing of society, through the virtues that come with a thorough education."[15] Reading such assertions, one may wonder to what degree they reflect the author's own views and to what extent they are designed to deflect criticism of her feminist activity.

The language and culture of Andean Indians are represented in *Birds without a Nest* with a thoroughness truly unusual for its time. One reason is that Matto, among Peruvian intellectuals of her day, was distinguished by her knowledge of the Quechua language and the culture of its speakers. As Berg notes, "She was brought up on a family estate nearby [El Cuzco] where she played with the Indian children and learned both Quechua and Spanish, thus beginning a familiarity with Quechua culture that would be of continuing importance to her."[16] By all accounts, Matto was exceptionally proficient in both speaking and reading Quechua. After her excommunication, Matto became associated to some degree with the American Bible Society. This Protestant group had as its principal mission the spread of the New Testament, and especially the Gospels, among new populations. The organization published Matto's Quechua translations of the four Gospels and the Acts of the Apostles.

Birds without a Nest is, among other things, an effort to educate non-Indian readers about native communities. A number of Quechua words appear in the text. In some cases Matto relied on the reader's knowledge or on context to provide a meaning, but in others she provided a definition. (While the English translator favored parenthetical translations, Matto placed a small glossary at the back of the novel, a practice taken up by many subsequent *indigenista* novelists.) The use of occasional words and phrases in an indigenous language later came to be considered a rather crude way of representing Indian language in a Spanish American novel. Matto's introduction of Quechua cannot compete for complexity with, for example, the subtle Quechua flavoring of José María Arguedas's celebrated novel of 1958, *Los ríos profundos* (*Deep Rivers*, 1978); yet for its historical moment it is progressive. Matto was a nationalist in literary and cultural matters, dedicated to producing "Peruvian literature," to cite the closing words of her preface. She was determined to bring the major issues facing Peru, such as the dual linguistic situation of the country, to the attention of her readers.

Beyond Quechua vocabulary, Matto includes in her novel many references to indigenous Andean handicrafts, popular narratives and beliefs, music, and ceremonial customs. Notably, she also shows that non-Indian characters, including those who despise the native community, have adopted a few Quechua words and a number of indigenous folkways in dress, cuisine, and household decor. Lucia and Fernando appear as model Peruvians in part because of their eagerness to learn about the culture and the situation of the Indians they encounter. Matto sometimes uses Indian culture to add local color in a way that today seems superficial. But the author wrote in a period when local-color writing was not only in vogue, owing to Palma's success, but also esteemed as important to national literature.

Matto's outlook on native Andean culture was a mixture of assimilationism and cultural preservation. *Birds without a Nest* makes clear her desire to see the indigenous population achieve literacy in Spanish, receive the same education as non-Indian Peruvians, and make certain progressive changes in diet and living habits. At the same time, Matto wanted to maintain Quechua and to further its use as a written language. Of linguistic assimilationists, she wrote: "Those who advocate the extinction of Quechua are committing blasphemy against the ancient civilization of Peru and the modern need to learn about it." [17]

While *Birds without a Nest* is by far Matto's best-known novel, she went on to publish two related works of fiction, the 1892 *Indole* (Character) and *Herencia* (Heredity) from 1895. These two novels, especially the latter, are sometimes referred to as sequels to *Birds without a Nest*. Efraín Kristal sums up with greater precision the relation of Matto's three novels: "Although each novel can be read on its own, the plot lines of the three are interconnected, the central theme is shared, and the characters are informed by Manuel González Prada's political thought."[18] Though much less noted than *Birds without a Nest*, the two subsequent novels are today considered of greater value than the regionalist anecdotes and vignettes that form much of Matto's overall literary production.

A few words are in order concerning the English translation. *Birds without a Nest: A Story of Indian Life and Priestly Oppression in Peru* appeared in London in 1904, published by Charles J. Thynne and sponsored by the American Bible Society, with which, as noted, Matto had developed an association. The author's original preface was deleted and replaced with an introduction written by a representative of the society. Not too surprisingly, the new foreword suggested that the solution to the misbehavior of priests was not clerical reform but rather the replacement of Roman Catholicism with Protestantism in Spanish America. (In the present edition, the author's preface has been restored.)

The translation was credited to J.G.H.[19] When the translation is examined against the original, it is immediately evident that J.G.H. possessed an excellent knowledge of Spanish, including terms specific to the Andean region. J.G.H.'s English exhibits an elevated Victorian style well suited to the high register that Matto favored. Despite these virtues, J.G.H. took, on occasion, what would today be considered unacceptable license with the original text, bowdlerizing it as well as translating it. J.G.H.'s deletions are of several types. In many instances, the translator excised references to the human body; even descriptions of characters that dwell on their physical attractions are often severely cropped. In other cases, J.G.H. removed passages expressive of despair over social problems. The translator apparently disliked the cliff-hanging effect produced by cutting from one subplot to another and rearranged the chapters. The most drastic change is the elimination of an entire episode, that of the train derailment (restored in the present edition). The train wreck, which produces melodramatic suspense but scarcely furthers the plot, is probably the most complained-of feature of the plot.[20] Its suppression shows that J.G.H. was eager to improve the work.

Much more could be said about the complex relationship between the original and the translation, but it is more important to state the measures taken here to restore the text. I have rearranged the chapters in their original order, and where the translator suppressed words and phrases, and in some cases passages, I have supplied translations of my own, attempting to follow as closely as possible J.G.H.'s stylistic habits and elevated register. In restoring missing matter, I have utilized the edition published in Havana in 1974 by Casa de las Américas, the 1968 reissue by Las Américas Publishing Company of New York, and the 1889 edition by Félix Lajouans, Buenos Aires.

In a few cases, the translator's changes affect only the most superficial level of the text. For example, J.G.H. at times deletes such formulations as "said Don Fernando" or "replied Margarita" when it is evident which character has been speaking. The translator occasionally coalesces into a single summarizing phrase several descriptive details that are enumerated separately in the original. In this latter case, the summarized depictions represent a stylistic improvement over Matto's original feature-by-feature ones. As Brushwood puts it, "Clorinda Matto's concept of realism seems to demand . . . that she write certain descriptions in excruciating detail . . . . The details become especially overwhelming when the course of action is interrupted in favor of describing a lady's attire. There are paragraphs that sound something like the commentary at a fashion show."[21] In condensing via summary extremely detailed descriptions, J.G.H. has sacrificed none of the novel's semantic substance.

Readers approaching *Birds without a Nest* for the first time should bear in mind that Clorinda Matto was breaking new ground in Spanish American fiction as well as making her debut as a novelist. Such a close and personal view of Indian characters and life among native families had never before been attempted. It would be unfair to expect Matto to have fully worked out the novelistic structure and language that would best convey her vision. While *Birds without a Nest* may at times lack polish, it is rich in information and understanding. Matto brought to her best-known novel a knowing analysis of both racial relations and issues between the sexes. Her concept of companionship marriage (illustrated by Fernando and Lucia), her advocacy of women's education, and her beliefs about women's distinctive character reveal to today's readers the outlook of a nineteenth-century Spanish American feminist and progressive.

NOTES

1. Luis Mario Schneider, "Clorinda Matto de Turner," introduction to Matto, *Aves sin nido* (Buenos Aires: Félix Lajouane, 1889; reprint, New York: Las Américas, 1968), xxiv.

2. John S. Brushwood, "The Popular-Ethnic Sensitivity: Clorinda Matto de Turner's *Aves sin nido*," in his *Genteel Barbarism: New Readings of Nineteenth-Century Spanish-American Novels* (Lincoln: University of Nebraska Press, 1981), 139–157.

3. Ibid., 145.

4. Schneider, "Clorinda Matto de Turner," xx–xxi, cites as earlier *indigenista* novels *El padre Horán* (1848) by Narciso Aréstegui and *La trinidad del indio o costumbres del interior* (1885) by José T. Itolarres (pseudonym of José Torres y Lara), both obscure works unknown even to most specialists.

5. Schneider, "Clorinda Matto de Turner," xxiii.

6. Manuel González Prada repeatedly pointed to judges, priests, and town governors as the principal oppressors of the Andean Indians. The original formulation of this triad is often attributed to a controversial speech delivered by González Prada in the Teatro Politeama de Lima on 29 July 1888.

7. Antonio Cornejo Polar, *La novela peruana: Siete estudios.* (Lima: Editorial Horizonte, 1977), 18.

8. Concha Meléndez, "*Aves sin nido*, por Clorinda Matto de

Turner," in her *La novela indianista en Hispanoamérica* (1934; rpt. Río Piedras: Universidad de Puerto Rico, 1961), 177–184.

9. Cornejo Polar, *La novela peruana*, 17.

10. Cornejo Polar, "Prólogo," *Aves sin nido* (Havana: Casa de las Américas, 1974), xvii–xviii.

11. Ibid., xvii. Cornejo Polar sees the uneasy coexistence of romanticism and naturalism as the source of many inconsistencies in *Birds without a Nest*.

12. Mary G. Berg, "Clorinda Matto de Turner (1852–1909), Peru," in *Spanish American Women Writers: A Bio-Bibliographical Source Book*, ed. Diane E. Marting (Westport, Connecticut: Greenwood Press, 1990), 304.

13. Berg, "Writing for Her Life: The Essays of Clorinda Matto de Turner," in *Reinterpreting the Spanish American Essay: Women Writers of the Nineteenth and Twentieth Centuries*, ed. Doris Meyer (Austin: University of Texas Press, 1995), 80–89, is especially concerned with Matto's vision of women in society. See also Berg, "Clorinda Matto de Turner," 303–315.

14. Clorinda Matto de Turner made these statements in the speech "Light amidst the Darkness," which she delivered on the occasion of her reception into the Ateneo de Lima, an influential circle of Peruvian intellectuals, on 6 January 1887. They appear in Schneider, "Clorinda Matto de Turner," xvii.

15. Clorinda Matto de Turner, *Elementos de Literatura: Según el Reglamento de Instrucción Pública. Para el Uso del Bello Sexo* (Arequipa, Peru: Imprenta La Bolsa, 1886); cited in Schneider, "Clorinda Matto de Turner," xvii.

16. Berg, "Writing for Her Life," 80–81.

17. Clorinda Matto de Turner, *Leyendas y recortes* (Lima: Imprenta La Equitativa, 1893); cited in Schneider, "Clorinda Matto de Turner," xxxv.

18. Efraín Kristal, "Clorinda Matto de Turner," in *Latin American Writers*, ed. Carlos A. Solé and Maria Isabel Abreu (New York: Scribner's, 1989), 1, 306.

19. Berg, "Clorinda Matto de Turner," 305 and 313, identifies the translator as J. H. Hudson, although the source of this attribution does not appear in her article.

20. Cornejo Polar, "Prólogo," xv, writes that the train derailment "has no other function than to create suspense and anxiety
in the reader." Brushwood, "Popular-Ethnic Sensitivity," 144,
though granting that the incident may illustrate the isolation of
Peru's small towns, finds relatively little significance in this subplot.

21. Brushwood, "Popular-Ethnic Sensitivity," 143–144.

BIRDS
WITHOUT
A NEST

AUTHOR'S PREFACE

If history is the mirror wherein generations to come shall contemplate the image of generations that went before, the novel must be the photograph that records the vices and virtues of a people, along with a moral prescription for the former and an admiring homage to the latter.

That is what gives such importance to the novel of local customs, whose pages often contain the secret to the reform of certain human types, if not their extinction.

In countries in which, as in ours, Literature is still in its infancy, the novel must exert greater influence in moderating widespread patterns of conduct. Consequently, when there appears a work whose vision rises above those regions in which is born and dies the novel whose plot is purely amorous or escapist, one may well call upon its reading public to reach out a hand and give it to the people.

Who knows whether, after turning the last page of this book, readers will recognize the importance of careful selection and oversight of the authorities, both civil and ecclesiastic, who preside over the destinies of those who live in the isolated towns in the interior of Peru?

Who knows whether they will recognize the need for a married clergy, as a social necessity?

Acting upon this hope, I have been inspired to take exact likenesses and have drawn my portraits from life, presenting the copy to the reader for judgment.

I love the native race with a tender love, and so I have observed its customs closely, enchanted by their simplicity, and, as well, the abjection into which this race is plunged by small-town despots, who, while their names may change, never fail to live up to the epithet of tyrants. They are no other than, in general, the priests, governors, caciques, and mayors.

Moved by this affection, I have observed over fifteen years a multitude of episodes that, had they transpired in Switzerland, Provence, or the Savoy, would find some voice to sing of them, their novelist or their historian, who would immortalize them with the lyre or the pen. Yet in the isolation of my home country, they are fortunate to be committed to the pale, pencilled notes of a sister.

I repeat that, in submitting my work to the reader's judgment, I do so with the hope that this judgment takes into account the idea of improving conditions in Peru's small towns; and even should it not reach beyond simple commiseration, the author of these pages will have achieved her aim, by reminding readers that in this country there are brothers who suffer, exploited in the night of ignorance, reduced to martyrdom in that darkness that cries out for light; by drawing attention to points of no slight importance for the nation's progress; and by *making*, at the same time, Peruvian literature.

**Clorinda
Matto de Turner**

To Manuel González Prada

PART ONE

1
THE
TOWN
OF KILLAC

It was a cloudless summer morning, and all Nature, smiling in her felicity, sent up a hymn of adoration to the author of her beauty.

The heart, tranquil as the nest of the dove, gave itself up to the contemplation of the magnificent picture.

The single plaza of the little Peruvian town of Killac measures three hundred and fourteen square metres. Buildings of different kinds are grouped around it, the red tiled roofs of the houses rising above the straw-thatched cabins of the Indians.

On the left rises that common home of the Christian—the temple, surrounded by a stone wall, and in the belfry, where the old bell laments for those who die and laughs for the newly born, the cullcus build their nests.

The cemetery of the church is the place where the people gather together on Sundays after mass, comparing notes about their work, murmuring at their hardships, and gossiping a little about each other.

Less than half a mile to the south one finds a beautiful country house, noted for its elegant construction, contrasting strongly with the simplicity of its location. Its name is Manzanares. This was the property of the former priest of Killac, Don Pedro Miranda y Claro, afterwards Bishop of the Diocese, of whom careless-tongued people sometimes spoke in not very saintly terms when commenting upon occurrences which took place during the twenty years that Don Pedro was the shepherd of the flock. In that period Manzanares was built and became afterwards the summer residence of his Illustrious Highness.

The beautiful plain, surrounded by orchards and cultivated fields, watered by channels of murmuring crystal water, the river flowing near, all combine to render Killac a place of poetic beauty.

The night before, rain had fallen, accompanied by hail and thunder, clearing and refreshing the air, and the rising sun, peeping above the horizon, sent its golden rays over the trembling plants, turning into jewels the crystal drops not yet fallen from the green leaves.

The swallows and thrushes flew from treetop to house, filling the air with music, their bright plumage glittering in the sun.

Early summer mornings, bright and beautiful, inviting one to live, inspire the painter and the poet in the pleasant land of Perú.

2
THE
YUPANQUI
FAMILY

On that morning which we have described, when the sun, recently risen from his dark couch, called bird and flower to spring up to salute him with their homage of love and gratitude, a labourer crossed the plaza, guiding his yoke of oxen laden with the implements of husbandry, a yoke, a goad and leathern straps for work, and the provisions of the day; the traditional *chuspa*, or bag of woven wool of various colours, fastened to the belt containing the *coca* leaves and cakes of *llipta* for his lunch.

On passing the door of the temple he reverently lifted his cap and murmured something like an invocation, then went on his way, now and then looking back sorrowfully at the cabin from whence he came.

Was it fear or doubt, love or hope that troubled his soul at that moment? It was plainly to be seen that something impressed his mind strongly.

Above the stone wall that rose to the south of the plaza, a head showed and then, quick as a fox, hid again behind the stones, but not without revealing the handsome head of a

woman, whose black hair, long and straight, was divided in two,
making a frame for the beautiful bust of a woman with its
somewhat coppery skin, where the cheekbones stood out mark-
edly with their red hue, especially in the areas most abundantly
supplied with blood.

Scarcely was the labourer lost to sight on the far side of
Cañas when the head hidden behind the wall took on a body,
leaping over. It was a woman full of youthful vigour, who stood
out as an exemplar of Peruvian beauty. She had reached thirty,
but her freshness gave no hint she was over twenty-eight. She
wore a floating skirt of dark blue baize, and a bodice of brown
velveteen decorated at the collar and wrists with silver trim and
bone buttons was round her waist.

Shaking off her dress the mud which had fallen upon her
from the wall, she directed her steps to a modest-looking white
cottage with tiled roof not far away.

At the open door she was met by a young lady neatly dressed
in grey with lace trimmings and mother-of-pearl buttons who
was none other than the Señora Lucia, wife of Don Fernando
Marin, a gentleman who had some business connection with the
mines near the place and had settled temporarily in Killac.

The newcomer addressed Lucia quickly without ceremony,
saying: "In the name of the Virgin, señora, protect this day an
unfortunate family. He who has gone to the fields to-day passing by you here, laden with the implements of labor, is Juan
Yupanqui, my husband and father of our two little girls. Alas,
señora! He has gone out with his heart half dead, because he
knows that to-day will be the day of distribution, and as the
overseer directs the barley sowing he cannot hide himself because, besides the imprisonment, he would have to pay the fine,
and we have no money. I was crying beside Rosalia, who sleeps
by the fireplace, when suddenly my heart told me that you are
good, and without Juan's knowledge I came to implore your assistance for the sake of the Virgin, señora."

A flood of tears put an end to that supplication which was
full of mystery to Lucia, for, having resided but a few months in
the place, she was ignorant of its customs and could not appre-

ciate at their full value the references made by the poor woman, although they roused her sympathy.

It is necessary to see face to face these disinherited creatures, to hear from their own lips in their expressive language the narrative of their actual circumstances, in order to understand the quick sympathy which springs up unconsciously in noble hearts, and how they came to take part in their suffering finally, although at first only a desire for knowledge prompts them to observe folkways of which most Peruvians are ignorant, something that only a handful of people deplore.

The words of the Indian woman excited the interest of the sympathetic Lucia, and she asked kindly: "And who are you?"

"I am Marcela, my lady, the wife of Juan Yupanqui, poor and unprotected," replied the woman, drying her eyes upon the sleeve of her dress.

Lucia, putting her hand kindly upon her shoulder, invited her to take a seat upon a stone bench in the garden and rest herself. "Let us talk calmly," said Lucia, eager to learn all about Indian ways.

Marcela calmed her grief and, perhaps with the hope of salvation, responded precisely to Lucia's questions. She felt such trust that she would have told her even her reprehensible deeds, even those evil thoughts that, in humankind, are like the exhalation of vicious germs. So relaxed, she said: "As you are not of this place, señora, you do not know the martyrdom we suffer from collectors, overseers, and priests. Alas, alas! Why does not a plague carry us all away that we might at least sleep peacefully in the earth?"

"Why do you despair so, poor Marcela? There will be some remedy, you are a mother, and the heart of a mother lives as many lives in one as she has children."

"Yes, señora," replied Marcela. "You have the face of the Virgin to whom we offer our praise and prayers, and that is why I came to ask your help. I wish to save my husband. He said to me when he went away: 'One of these days I shall have to throw myself into the river, because I cannot endure this life; and I want to kill you too before giving my life to the water,' and you know, señora, that this is not right."

"It is a wrong thought, a crazy idea—poor Juan!" said Lucia
sadly; then casting a searching glance upon the woman continued: "And what is the most urgent need to-day? Speak freely,
Marcela."

"Last year," the woman said, "they left in our cabin ten dollars for two quintals of wool. This money we spent buying,
among other things, these clothes I am wearing, for Juan said we
would get together during the year as much more money; but
this has not been possible because of the *faena** and because my
mother-in-law died at Christmas time and the priest put an *embargo* upon our potato crop to pay the expenses of the burial and
prayers. Now I have to enter the parochial house of *mita,** leaving my husband and daughters; and while I am gone who knows
if Juan will not go crazy and die. Who knows, also, the fate that
awaits me, for the women who go to the *mita* come out—looking down at the ground."

"Enough! Do not tell me any more!" exclaimed Lucia, horror-
stricken at the depths to which the narration of Marcela was
leading her. The last words struck terror to the heart of the
pure-minded dove, who was finding civilised beings to be nothing but monsters of greed and even lust.

"I will speak to the Governor and the priest this very day,
and perhaps to-morrow you will remain free and contented. Go
now and take care of your little girls, and when Juan returns
soothe him—tell him that you have spoken to me, and tell him
to come and see me."

The poor woman gave a sigh of satisfaction, for the first time
in her life.

So solemn is the situation of one who, in the supreme hour
of misfortune, finds a generous heart to lend her aid, that the
heart does not know whether to bathe with tears or cover with
kisses in silence the loving hand stretched out to help, or to
break out in words of blessing. That is what passed during
those moments through the heart of Marcela.

---

* Obligatory and unpaid labour which the authorities impose upon the Indians.
* Unpaid and enforced work which the Indian women do in the houses of the
priests and authorities.

Those who do good to the down-trodden never can measure
the worth of one single word of kindness, one loving smile that
for the fallen, the unhappy, is like the rays of sunshine that return life to the members benumbed by the ice of misfortune.

3
INDIAN
LOANS,
FIVE
HUNDRED
PER CENT

In the Peruvian provinces, where
they breed the alpaca, and where
traffic in wool is the chief source of riches, there exists almost
without exception the custom known as "distribution in advance," which the business magnates, the well-to-do people of
the place, practise.

For the payment in advance which the wool buyers make and
force the Indians to accept, they fix the price of a quintal of
wool so low that the gain which the capital invested is made to
produce exceeds five hundred per cent. This usury, together
with the extortion that goes with it, virtually turns existence
into a hell for those barbarians.

The Indians who are owners of alpacas emigrate from their
huts during the time of distribution, in order not to receive the
money advanced, which for them is almost as cursed as the
thirty pieces of silver received by Judas.

But does the abandonment of home, the wanderings among
the mountains, ensure their safety? No.

The collector, who is at the same time the distributor or as-
sessor, breaks into their cabins, whose weak lock in the door
made of hide offers but little resistance, leaves upon a bench or
bunk the money, and marches off to return next year with the

list which is the only judge and witness for the unfortunate debtor.

When the year is finished the collector returns with a retinue of ten or twelve *mestizos,* sometimes disguised as soldiers, and with a special balance with counter weights of stone, takes out fifty pounds of wool for twenty-five. If the Indian secretes his wool, his only source of income, or if he protests and curses, he is subjected to such tortures as the pen refuses to narrate.

The pastoral of one of the most celebrated Bishops the Peruvian church ever had makes meritorious these excesses, but does not dare to speak of the cold-water enemas which in some places they employ to force the Indians to declare where they have hidden their goods. The Indian fears that even more than the lash. These inhuman beings who take the form for the spirit of the law allege that flogging is prohibited in Perú, but not the barbarities which they practise on their brothers in misfortune.

Oh! May God see fit one day, exercising His mercy, to decree the extinction of the Indian race, which after having shone in its imperial grandeur, drinks the mire of opprobrium. May such an extinction be God's will, since it is not possible for the Indians to regain their dignity, or to exercise their rights!

The bitter sorrow and despair of Marcela, when thinking of the near coming of the collector, was only the just and anguished explosion of one who sees before her only a world of poverty and infamous pain.

4

WHITE HOUSE

Lucia was no ordinary woman. She had received a good education, and by means of comparisons, her quick intelligence often reached the light of truth in advance of others. She was tall and graceful, not very fair, but what is called in the country "pearl-coloured"; her beautiful eyes were shaded by long lashes and velvety eyebrows; she had also that distinctively feminine charm, a wealth of long hair that, when let loose, cascaded down her back like an undulating, shimmering cloak of tortoise shell. She had not quite completed twenty summers, but marriage had set upon her that sign and seal of lady that so well becomes a young woman who understands how to unite amiability of character with seriousness of manner. Her husband, Don Fernando Marin, was the chief shareholder, and currently Director, of a company for working some silver mines in an adjoining province, and had his office in Killac. Here they had lived for a year in what was known as the White House.

After her interview with Marcela, Lucia set herself to work to form a plan for saving the poor woman from her painful situation. The word of her husband would have been sufficient to realize all immediate plans, but Don Fernando had gone on a visit to the mines and might not return for some weeks.

The first thought that came to her was to speak personally with the priest and the Governor. For that purpose she sent notes to each of them asking for the favour of a visit.

Arranging her reception room and putting things in order generally for the expected visit, Lucia seated herself on the sofa and began to form her plan of attack.

Presently a heavy knock aroused her from her meditations, and the softly opened door gave entrance to the priest and the Governor.

5
PRIEST
AND
GOVERNOR

Of low stature, flat head, large wide-open nose, thick lips, small grey eyes; a short neck surrounded by a band of black and white beads, unshaven chin, dressed in a habit of black cloth, badly cut and badly attended to, a hat of Guayaquil straw in his right hand—such was the aspect of the first personage who entered, whom Lucia saluted with much respect, saying, "May God be with you, Father Pascual."

The priest, Pascual Vargas, successor of Don Pedro Miranda y Claro, in the holy office at Killac, inspired from the first very serious doubts as to the idea of his having learned in the Seminary either Theology or Latin, a language that seemed out of place in his mouth, guarded by two walls of very large, white teeth. His age bordered on fifty years. His manner and appearance were such that it was not difficult to understand Marcela's reluctance to enter the parochial house in the role of *mita*, a house that, according to the native expression, women left with their eyes cast to the ground.

For an observer of physiological traits, Father Pascual's combined features could be summed up by a nest of lustful serpents, ready to awaken at the first sound of a woman's voice.

To the mind of Lucia came involuntarily the question as to how a person of such appearance and manner had been able to reach the position of the grandest of ministries, for in her religious convictions the priesthood was the embodiment of the highest, sublimest protectorship for man on earth, receiving him in the cradle with the sign of baptism, depositing his remains in the earth with the holy water of purification, and during his pilgrimage in this vale of sorrows sweetening and softening his bitter pain with the wise word of counsel and the soft voice of hope.

Lucia forgot that its being a mission dependent upon the human will explained its propensity to err; she had also very little idea of what the characters and lives of the priests in those retired places were.

The personage enveloped in a large Spanish cloak, who followed Father Pascual into the room, and whose name appears in fourteen wills, which could count as his titles, if not as his possessive family tree, was Don Sebastian Pancorbo, a name his Honour received in a solemn baptismal ceremony, with the cross on high, new robes, a silver sprinkler, and the voice of an organ, administered three days after his birth.

Don Sebastian, who cuts quite an original figure, judging from the way he dresses, is tall and bony; his face never suffers those masculine inconveniences, beard and moustache; his dark, lively, greedy eyes look off toward the left, and it is clear he is not indifferent to the sound of metal or the metal of a female voice. The little finger of his right hand had become twisted when he was young, when he struck a friend, and ever since he had worn a half glove woven of vicuña, although he could use that hand with a peculiar grace. The man had not an atom of triglycerine in his blood; he seemed made for peace, but his genial weakness often landed him in ridiculous situations that his companions played to the hilt. He was known for strumming the guitar in a tone-deaf, clumsy way, even though he drank like a member of an army band.

Don Sebastian, after passing three years in a primary school in a neighbouring city, returned to his native town, married Doña Petronila Hinojosa, daughter of one of the notables of the place, and was immediately made Governor; that is to say, he arrived at the highest post known and aspired to in a small town.

These two grand personages seated themselves comfortably in the arm chairs indicated by Lucia.

The Señora Marin set herself to the task of interesting her callers in favour of Marcela. Addressing herself particularly to the priest, she said: "In the name of the Christian religion, which is pure love, tenderness, and hope; in the name of your Master, who commanded us to give to the poor, I ask you, Father, to pardon this debt which weighs upon the family of Juan Yupanqui. Ah! You will have in exchange double treasure in heaven!"

"Señora," replied the priest, settling himself comfortably and resting both hands upon the arms of the chair, "all this is beautiful nonsense, but, God help us, who lives without income? Today, with the increase of ecclesiastical taxes, and the rush of civilised people who will come with the railroads, our emoluments will cease; and . . . , and . . . in short, Doña Lucia, away with the priests! We will starve to death!"

"Has the Indian Yupanqui come for this?" interposed the Governor in support of the priest, and with a triumphant tone concluded, emphasising the words for Lucia's benefit: "You know, señora, that custom is law and no one can take us out of our customs."

"Gentlemen, charity is also a law of the heart," interrupted
Lucia.

"And Juan, eh? We will see if he will return to touch these
springs again, this mischief-making Indian," continued Pancorbo
in a threatening tone that could not help being noticed by Lucia, whose heart trembled with fear.

The words exchanged between them made perfectly clear to
Lucia the moral degradation of these men, from whom nothing could be hoped and everything was to be feared. Her plan
was frustrated completely, but her heart remained fully interested in the family of Marcela, and she was resolved to protect
them against all abuse. Her dove's heart felt its own self-respect
wounded, and her brow grew pale.

She spoke up energetically: "A sad reality, sirs! I shall have to
persuade myself that vile self-interest has withered also the most
beautiful flowers of the sentiment of humanity in these regions
where I thought to find patriarchal families with the love of
brother for brother. We have asked nothing of anyone, and the
family of Juan Yupanqui will never solicit either your favour or
your protection." On uttering these words with all the warmth
of a generous heart, the beautiful eyes of Lucia were directed,
with the look of one giving a command, towards the open door.

The two potentates of Killac were confounded by this unexpected outburst of Lucia, and seeing no other way of saving
themselves, took up their hats to retire.

"Señora Lucia, do not be offended by this, and believe me to
be always your faithful chaplain," said Don Pascual; while Don
Sebastian hastened to remark dryly: "Good afternoon, Señora
Lucia."

Lucia cut short the usual ceremony of leave-taking, simply
inclining her head in response.

Seeing those men go away leaving such a deep impression on
her pure soul, she said to herself, tremblingly but vehemently:
"Oh no, no! That man insults the Catholic priesthood! I have
seen in the city superior beings with grey heads go in silence and
quietness to look after the poor and the orphan, to succour and
console them. I have contemplated the Catholic priest at the
bedside of the dying; have seen him pure before the altar of

sacrifice; weeping and humble in the home of the widow and orphan; have seen him take the last loaf of bread from his table
and give it to the poor, depriving himself of sustenance and
thanking God for the mercy that he could give! But that priest
Pascual—is he one of those? No. A priest of wickedness instead. And that other—his soul cast in the narrow mould of
avarice; the Governor does not merit the dignity which has been
given him as though he were an honest man. Out of here, all of
you, I can do it myself—beg my Fernando, and bring into our
home the flowers of satisfaction!"

Five peals of the family clock made Lucia realise how much
time had gone by and announced to her that dinner was served.

The wife of Señor Marin, her cheeks ablaze with the fire of
indignation she harboured, made her way down several hallways
and came to the dining-room, where she took her usual seat.

The ceiling and walls of the dining-room of the White
House were stained an oak colour; here and there hung elegant
oil paintings, representing a half-plucked partridge or a hare
readied for the stew pot. On the left side of the front wall was a
serving table with mirrors that reflected the utensils symmetri-
cally placed there. To the right were two smaller tables, one with
a chessboard and one with a roulette wheel; that was where the
employees of the mining company liked to spend their free
time. The dining table, set in the centre of the room, covered
with extremely white, well-ironed tablecloths, displayed country-
style tableware, all of blue china embellished in red.

The soup gave off a thick steam whose fragrance bespoke a
creamy, chunky meat *cuajada*, made from ground beef together
with spices, nuts, and dumplings, swimming in a broth of *aguado;*
this was followed by three hearty dishes, among them that rustic corn delight, *locro colorado.*

As Lucia was being served Carabaya coffee, clear, hot, and
strong, exuding an inspiring aroma from inside porcelain cups, a
boy came with a letter. Recognizing the handwriting of her husband, she opened it immediately, and, as she read, an observer
would have known, by the brightening up of her expressive
countenance, that it brought her good news. Señor Marin wrote
that he would be with her the next morning, as the constantly

falling masses of ice and snow from the mountains had interrupted the work among the mines for a time.

6
JUAN'S
RETURN
HOME

When Marcela returned to her cabin, carrying a world of hope in her heart, she found her children awake and the youngest crying disconsolately at finding her mother absent.

A little patting from her mother, and a handful of boiled corn to eat, was sufficient to calm the grief of the innocent creature who, although born in poverty and rags in the hut of an Indian, shed the same crystal tears as those that fall from the eyes of the children of kings.

Marcela took up with enthusiasm the *tocarpus* that held her portable loom; with the help of her elder daughter she set it up in the middle of the room, preparing the threads of the background and the figure, to continue the weaving of a beautiful poncho, patterned with all the colours the Indians use, combining Brazil wood, cochineal, annatto dye, and the yellow flowers of the *quico.*

Never had she begun her daily task more contentedly, and never built more castles in the air than now as she mediated how best to impart to Juan the good news that awaited him.

The hours, for this same reason, seemed very long; but at last came the evening twilight, enveloping in its shadows valley and town, calling away from the fields the cooing doves, which circled around in different directions in quest of their protecting tree.

With these came Juan, and no sooner had Marcela heard his step in the distance, than she went out to meet him; helped him to tie the oxen in the yard and threw food in the manger. When at last Juan was seated in the house she began to talk to him with a certain timidity, as if doubting how he would receive the news she had to give him.

"Do you know the lady Lucia, Juan?" she asked.

"I go to mass, Marcela, and there everyone is known," replied Juan with indifference.

"Well, I have spoken with her to-day."

"You? And for what?" inquired the Indian in surprise, looking intently at his wife.

"I am so pained by all we have to endure; you have made me see plainly that this life is making you desperate."

"Did the collector come?" interrupted Juan.

Marcela replied calmly and confidently: "Not yet, thank Heaven, but hear me, Juan. I believe that good señora can relieve us; she told me that she would help us and that you must go and see her."

"Poor flower of the desert, Marcela," said the Indian, shaking his head and taking up the little Rosalia clinging to his knees, "Your heart is like the fruit of the *penca,* break off one and another comes to take its place. I am older than you and I have wept without hope."

"Not so I, although you tell me I imitate the *tuna;* but better thus than to be as you are, like the *mastuerzo* which, once touched, withers away. The hand of some evil spirit has touched you; but I have seen the face of the Virgin, the same, the very same, as the face of the Señora Lucia," said Marcela, laughing like a little girl.

"It may be," said the sad-hearted Juan, "but I come tired out from work and without bringing one loaf of bread for you, who are *my virgin;* and for these little chickens," pointing to the two little girls.

"You complain too much, Juan; perhaps you do not remember that when the priest goes to his house with his pockets full of silver from the responses of All Saints, there is no one waiting for him as I wait for thee, with open arms, and with kisses of love such as the little angels keep for thee. Ungrateful! Thinking of bread; here we have cold boiled corn and cooked corn meal, which with its appetising odour is inviting us—eat, ungrateful one!"

Marcela was changed. The hopes that Lucia had raised in her heart made her another person; and her logic, mixed with the voice of the heart, was irresistible and convincing.

Juan drew his daughter to his side, Marcela took from the fire two earthen pots, and all partook of the frugal repast.

The supper was finished and the house already enveloped in the dark shades of night. Without other light than that of the soft flame made by some little half-burnt sticks in the fire, they all went to rest in one common bed made on a wide brick platform; a hard bed, but one which, for the love and resignation of the family, had the softness of feathers which love has let fall from his white wings. A bed of roses, where love, like the primitive sentiment of tenderness, lives still, without the uncertainties and the midnight mysteries that the city talks about in hushed tones, without managing to keep them secret.

With the morning light the family left their humble bed, offered the prayer of praise and thanksgiving, made the sign of the cross on their brows and began the labours of the new day.

Marcela was the first to say: "Juan, I am going over soon to see the Señora Lucia. You are unbelieving and taciturn, but my heart is speaking to me without ceasing since yesterday."

"Go, then, Marcela, go; because to-day the collector will not fail to come. I have dreamed it, and we have no other resource," answered the Indian, whose spirits seemed to have revived somewhat under the influence of his wife's words.

7
FERNANDO'S
GIFT
TO LUCIA

That morning the White House seemed full of happiness. The return of Don Fernando brought infinite happiness to his home, where he was both loved and respected.

Lucia, strongly determined to find some positive means of carrying out the purpose in regard to the family of Yupanqui, resolved to take advantage of the poetry and sweetness which surround the meeting of husband and wife after a separation.

Lucia, who some hours before seemed languid and sorrowful like flowers without sun or dew, had become strong and cheerful in the arms of the man who had confided to her keeping the sanctity of his home, and his name, the holy ark of his honour, in calling her wife.

The chain of flowers which unite two wills in one, bound together the husband and wife, or God whose name is love, the God of Love, himself welding the links.

"Fernando, soul of my soul," said Lucia, putting her hands upon her husband's shoulders, and leaning her forehead somewhat flirtatiously against his chin, "I am going to collect a debt, executively."

"You are quite a lawyer to-day, my dear. Speak, but remember that if the debt is not legally correct you will pay me a fine," replied her husband, smiling.

"A fine! That is what you exact always. I will pay the fine. What I wish you to remember is a solemn promise which you have made me for the twenty-eighth of July."

"The twenty-eighth of July?"

"You pretend to forget; do you not remember you promised me a velvet dress to display in the city?"

"Perfectly, my dear, and I will fulfil my promise. I will order it by the first post. How fine you will be with that dress!"

"No, no, Fernando; what I wish is that you permit me to dispose of the value of the dress, on condition that I present myself on the twenty-eighth of July as elegantly dressed as you have seen me since our marriage."

"And what—?"

"Nothing; I will not admit any questions; say yes or no!" and the lips of Lucia met those of Don Fernando, who, satisfied and happy, replied: "Flatterer! What can I deny you when you speak to me thus? How much do you need for this caprice?"

"Very little; two hundred dollars."

"Very well," said her husband, tearing a leaf out of his note-
book and writing upon it; "Here you have an order for the cashier
of the Company to pay you two hundred dollars. And now let
me go to work to make up for the time lost by the journey."

"Thank you, thank you, Fernando," she said, taking the paper, happy as a child.

Leaving the room Don Fernando went to his office, his mind
full of pleasant thoughts awakened by that girlish petition of
Lucia, comparing it with the useless expenditures with which
other women victimise their husbands in their desire for show
and luxury, and this comparison convinced him the more of the
value of good habits inculcated in a child in the paternal home.
The Peruvian woman is docile and virtuous as a general rule.

Shortly after the departure of Don Fernando, Marcela entered the yard of the White House accompanied by a young
girl. This child was a wonder of beauty and grace, which from
the first interested Lucia, awakening a desire to see the father,
because her rare beauty was a striking example of the loveliness
often produced by the mixture of Spanish and Peruvian blood
so often seen in this country.

Looking closely at the girl, Lucia said to herself: "This will
be, without doubt, the good angel of Marcela, because God has
put a peculiar brilliance in those countenances from which looks
out a privileged soul."

8
DANGER
AHEAD When the priest and the
Governor left the house of the
Señora Marin after the interview in which she tried to influence
them in favour of the family of Yupanqui, a lively conversation
ensued as they went their way down the street.

"Here's a pretty state of things! What do you think, Don Sebastian, of the pretensions of that señora?" said the priest, taking out a cigar and preparing it for lighting.

"That was the only thing wanting, Father, that some foreigners should come here to make rules for us, modifying the customs which have existed from the time of our great-grandfathers," answered the Governor, stopping a moment to wrap himself up in his great cape, while the priest added, "Give a little more rope to these Indians and soon we shall not have anyone even to draw up water to wash out the cups."

"We must get rid of these foreigners, really, Father, for these Indians, if they have anyone to uphold them, will soon become insufferable."

"That is just what I was going to suggest to you, Governor. Here, among ourselves in family, we get along beautifully; but these foreigners come here to observe us, to watch us, even to our manner of eating—if we have a clean tablecloth, if we eat with spoons or with sticks," grumbled the priest, sending out a cloud of smoke from his mouth.

"Do not trouble yourself, Father; let us be united, and the occasion for throwing them out of the town will soon present itself."

"But with great caution, Don Sebastian; we must be very careful in these matters, these people are well connected and we might make a false move."

"We know what they are working for. Do you remember what Don Fernando said one day?"

"Certainly, Governor; he wishes that the 'distributions' should be suppressed; says that they are an injustice! Ha! ha! ha!" laughed the priest maliciously, throwing away the stump of his cigar.

"He also wishes that the poor should have free burials, and that even debts should be pardoned. Fine times for free burials! Really, Father," added Don Sebastian, whose eternal "really" caused one to suspect him to be either a hypocrite or an idiot.

When they arrived at the Governor's house, he invited the priest to enter. Here they found a number of the most notable people gathered together commenting upon the fact of the priest

and Governor being called to the house of the Señora Marin,
the news having already been spread all over the town.

When the two important personages entered, everyone rose
to his feet to salute them, and the Governor immediately ordered a bottle of the "pure article."

"It is necessary, Father, to drown the fly with a little drink,
really," said Don Sebastian, meaningly, taking off his great cape.

"Certainly, my good Sebastian, and you always have the
best," answered the priest, rubbing his hands.

"Yes, Father, it is of the best, really, because Doña Rufa sends
it to me before baptizing it."

At that moment a *pongo** entered with a bottle of alcohol and
a glass.

The furniture of the drawing-room, typical of the place, consisted of two large sofas covered with black oil cloth nailed on
with round brass tacks, some wooden chairs, the backs of which
were painted with flowers and fruit. In the centre of the room
was a round table covered with a green cloth on which were
materials for writing. The walls were adorned with illustrated
papers showing a rare collection of personages, animals, and
landscapes of European countries. The floor was covered with
matting.

The gathering consisted of eight persons: the priest and the
Governor; Estéfano Benites, a young man with quick wit who,
having improved the hours of school to better advantage than
his schoolfellows, is already an important personage in this
small town; and five more individuals belonging to distinguished families of the place; all men of position, from having
contracted matrimony at the age of nineteen, the usual age in
these towns.

Estéfano Benites, who had passed his twenty-two years be-
neath the sun, was very tall and singularly thin, his wax-like pal-
lidness of countenance a very unusual thing in the place where
he was born, reminding one of the fatal consumption that attacks so many in the tropical countries.

* One who is obliged to give gratuitous service at the houses of the priests
and of the authorities.

Estéfano took the bottle left on the table by the *pongo* and served each one his respective glass of alcohol.

After the usual ration of two glasses, the appetite was really opened and the bottles kept coming in at the command of Don Sebastian.

The priest and the Governor were seated together on one of the sofas conversing privately, while the others were talking freely, gathered together in groups in different parts of the room.

But as confidence resides in the depth of the bottle, Don Sebastian soon found his tongue loosened, being well moistened by the "pure article," and began to talk openly.

"We must not consent, by any means, señor priest, really. And what do these gentlemen say?" raising his voice and striking the back of the seat with the glass he had just emptied.

"Chist!" said the priest, taking out a large black and white handkerchief and pretending to sneeze.

"Of what are you speaking, gentlemen?" asked Estéfano; and everyone turned towards the priest.

The priest Pascual put on a certain air of gravity and said: "The fact that the Señora Lucia called us there to speak to us about some poor scheming Indians who do not wish to pay what they owe; she has used words that, as Don Sebastian says, if understood by the Indians would destroy for us our customs of *repartos, mitas, pongos,* and everything else."

"We will never consent. What an idea!" shouted Estéfano supported by the others, while Don Sebastian added maliciously: "And has proposed free burial for the poor, and so, really, you see how our priest would suffer."

"Away with the pretensions of these foreigners!" shouted Estéfano, in the name of all.

"Once for all, let us put an end to all these evil teachings; it is necessary to expel from the place every foreigner who does not come with desires to support our customs, because we, really, are the children of the country," said Don Sebastian, raising his voice and going to the table to serve a glass to the priest.

"Yes, we are in our own country."

"Born in the land!"

"Genuine Peruvians!"

Such were the exclamations from all sides; but no one
stopped to inquire if the Marins were not Peruvians because
born in the capital.

"Carefully, carefully, say nothing, but work!" added the priest.

And that afternoon, in the house of the civil authority and
in the presence of the ecclesiastical ruler, was stirred up and
set to work the odium which was to envelop the honest Don
Fernando in a wave of blood, because of the kindly and charitable act of his wife.

9
A
STRATAGEM

When Marcela and the little
girl came near, Lucia exclaimed
in surprise: "Is this your daughter?"

"Yes, señora, she is fourteen years old; her name is Margarita
and she is to be your godchild," replied the Indian woman.

The reply was given with such an air of satisfaction, that
anyone seeing and hearing her would feel intuitively that this
woman was bathing herself in the perfume of holy pride which
overwhelms a mother when she understands that her daughters
are admired. Holy pride of motherhood which honours the
brow of woman, let it be in the city glowing with electric lights,
or in the humble town illuminated only by the melancholy traveller of night.

"Well, Marcela, you have done well in bringing that pretty
girl to see me. I am very fond of children; they are so innocent
and pure."

"Señora, it is because your soul is blossoming for heaven,"
said Marcela, more and more charmed at having gained the protection of such an angel of kindness.

"Have you spoken to Juan? How much money do you need
to pay all and live in peace?" asked Lucia.

"Alas, señora! I hardly know how to count it. Without doubt
it will be a great deal of money, because the collector, even if he

allows us to return the *reparto* in money, will ask for each quintal of wool sixty dollars, and in two there would be," and Marcela commenced to count on her fingers, but Lucia, shortening the arithmetical operation, said: "One hundred and twenty."

"Well then, señora, one hundred and twenty, ah! how much money!"

"How much did you tell me that they advanced you?"

"Ten dollars, señora."

"Then for ten dollars they exact now one hundred and twenty? Inhuman creatures!"

As she spoke Marcela's husband Juan ran up excitedly. Entering without ceremony he threw himself at Lucia's feet. Marcela sprang up and Lucia exclaimed: "What is the matter with you? What has happened?"

And the poor Indian, between sobs and fatigue, could hardly gasp out: "My daughter, señora! The collector!"

Marcela, beside herself with terror, on comprehending the import of these words, fell on her knees exclaiming: "Mercy, señora, mercy. The collector has carried off my daughter, my little one, because he did not find the wool! Ay, ay!"

"Inhuman, merciless men!" exclaimed Lucia, unable to understand the degree of inhumanity shown by these dishonest dealers. Giving her hand to the afflicted parents, she tried to calm them, saying in kindly tones: "But if they have only taken away the child, why do you despair so? They will soon return her. Juan will take them the money; all will be arranged in peace and he will praise God for consenting to the evil that we may better appreciate the good. Be calm!"

"No, señora, no!" replied the Indian, a little recovered from his confusion, "Because if we go late we will never see our daughter again. Here they sell them to the Majeños* and they are taken to Arequipa."

"Great God! Is it possible!" exclaimed Lucia, raising her hands to heaven.

At that moment the noble figure of Don Fernando appeared at the door in time to hear the last words of his wife, and hesi-

---

* Traders from the Valley of Majes who deal in liquors.

tated a little when he saw the faces of the Indians surrounding
Lucia, who, when she saw him, threw herself into his arm saying: "Fernando, Fernando mine; we cannot live here, and if you
insist we will live fighting the bloody battle of the good against
the bad. Oh, let us save them! Look at these unfortunate parents. It was to help them that I asked you for the two hundred
dollars, but before I could make use of the money their youngest daughter has been carried away to be sold. Oh, Fernando,
help me, because you believe in God, and God ordains charity
before everything else."

"Señor!" (Sir!)

"*Wiracocha!*" (Sir!) cried Juan and Marcela with one voice,
wringing their hands, while Margarita cried in silence.

"Do you know where the collector carried your daughter?"
inquired Don Fernando, turning to Juan and trying to hide his
feelings, for he was not ignorant of the means employed by
those men to gain their ends.

"Yes, señor, they have gone to the Governor," replied Juan.

"Well then, let us go. Follow me," ordered Don Fernando
with manifest resolution, and he went out followed by Juan.
Marcela was going to rush after them with Margarita, but Lucia
detained her, saying:

"Poor mother, do not go; offer your pain to the author of
resignation. Your affairs will be arranged to-day; I offer it, to
you in memory of my blessed mother. Sit down. How much do
you owe the priest?"

"For the interment of my mother-in-law—forty dollars,
señora."

"And for that he put an embargo on your potato crop?"

"No, señora, for the revenue."

"For the revenue? Then you would have remained debtors
eternally?"

"So it is, señora; but death can also play with the priest, for I
have seen many priests die and sleep in 'holy ground' without
collecting their debts," replied Marcela, recovering gradually her
attitude.

The simple philosophy of the Indian woman and her ideas of
compensation made Lucia smile. Calling a servant, she gave him

a written order telling him to bring the money immediately. She gave a glass of wine to Marcela and a slice of bread to Margarita, saying:

"You like sweet things, do you not? This is sweet bread with cinnamon; it is very nice."

Presently the servant returned with the money, and Lucia, taking forty dollars, gave them to Marcela saying:

"Take these, go, pay your debt to the priest. Do not speak of what has happened with the collector. If anyone asks you where this money came from, say to them that a Christian gave it to you in the name of God, and nothing more. Do not stay; try to return soon."

Such were the emotions of Marcela that her hand trembled so she could hardly count the money, letting it fall, piece by piece, from one hand to the other.

10
ROSALIA
RESTORED

If we attack the vices and evil habits of a people without having first laid the foundation of good instruction based on the belief in a Supreme Being, we shall see rise up an impregnable wall of selfish resistance, and shall behold the peaceable lambs of night transformed into ravenous wolves.

If we say to the cannibals that they must not eat the flesh of their prisoners, without having first given them some notions of humanity, of fraternal love and the dignity with which man respects the rights of other men, we shall probably very soon become ourselves food for these savages. We may judge that it is only a modified form of that same savage instinct which prompted that which occurred in Killac, and in all the small country places in the interior of Peru, where the scarcity of schools, the lack of good faith among the priests and the manifest depravity of those who traffic with ignorance and the consequent submission of the masses, each day remove those places farther away from true civilisation, which, once the groundwork is laid, will add to the country important sectors with the potential to build it up to greatness.

Don Fernando presented himself with Juan at the house of the Governor, who, surrounded by a crowd of people, was dispatching affairs of what he called "highest importance." The people filed away quietly one by one, until Pancorbo and Señor Marin were left alone.

Near the door of the house was a trembling little girl who, on seeing Juan enter, rushed to him as if pursued by a pack of hounds.

Don Fernando entered, serious and thoughtful. He was dressed in a suit of fine cassimire cut to perfection by the most famous tailor in Arequipa.

Don Fernando Marin was a distinguished person in the social circles of the Peruvian capital, and his physiognomy indicated a man with a sense of justice, an enlightened outlook, and both prudence and wisdom. On the tall side, with regular features and a fair complexion, he wore full sideburns, kept tidy by frequent combing and oiling. He had pale green eyes, a broad open brow, and slightly curly hair, carefully combed.

Taking off his hat politely as he entered the Governor's office, he extended his hand and said: "Excuse me, Don Sebastian, if I interrupt your work, but the fulfilment of a duty of humanity brings me to solicit of you that this man's little daughter, who has been taken, without doubt, as security for a debt, be restored to him and the author of this crime punished."

"Take a seat, Don Fernando, and let us talk at our ease. These Indians must not hear these things, really," responded Don Sebastian, seating himself nearer Don Fernando and speaking in a low voice. "It is true they have taken away the little girl; she is here, but, really, this is only a stratagem to oblige them to pay for some alpaca which they owe for a year now."

"But they have assured me, Señor Governor, that this debt comes from some ten dollars which were arbitrarily left in their house last year, and now they are desired to pay for two quintals of wool, the value of which is about one hundred and twenty dollars," replied Don Fernando seriously.

"Do you not know that this is the custom, and a legitimate business? Really, I advise you not to uphold these Indians," argued Pancorbo.

"But, Don Sebastian—"

"And finally, to make everything clear, this money belongs to Don Claudio Paz."

"Señor Paz is my friend; I will speak with him."

"That is another thing; so, really, for the present we have finished," said Don Sebastian, rising from his seat.

"No, señor, I wish you to have the little girl returned to her father. Will you accept my word for the money?"

"Certainly, certainly, Don Fernando, they shall give the little girl to Juan, and you will sign a paper," replied Don Sebastian, going to the table, and taking a sheet of paper put it before the other, saying: "This is not from want of confidence, but, really, it is necessary; you know the saying, that strict accounts preserve friendship."

Don Fernando went to the table, wrote a few lines, signed them, and passed the paper to Don Sebastian, who, adjusting his spectacles, read it over carefully, then folding and putting it into his pocket, he turned to Don Fernando and said:

"Very well, really, everything is arranged, Señor Marin; my respects to Señora Lucia."

"Thank you. Good-day," replied Don Fernando politely, giving his hand to the Governor, and as he went out, he shook off the dust of that manufactory of abuses. With him went Juan carrying little Rosalia in his arms.

Scarcely had Don Fernando left the office of the Governor, when the wife of the latter came in, and taking him by the arm very firmly said:

"I cannot endure it any longer, Sebastian; you will make me as miserable as the wife of Pilate, condemning so many just people and scrawling on so much paper that you had better let alone."

"Woman!" said Don Sebastian roughly; but she continued:

"I understand just what you are all making up against poor Don Fernando and his family, and I ask you to leave it off; leave it for God's sake, Sebastian. Remember that our son would be ashamed to-morrow."

"Leave off, woman, you are always with these songs. Really, women should never mix themselves up with men's business; they had better keep to their needles and pots and pans," answered her husband angrily. But Doña Petronila continued:

"Yes, that is what they all say to hush up the voice of their own heart and good counsel, throwing to one side all healthy advice. Remember, Sebastian," she added, striking the table with the palm of her hand as she went out with a disdainful glance at her husband.

"Puff," roared Don Sebastian, and he proceeded calmly to roll up a cigarette.

11
DOÑA
PETRONILA

Doña Petronila Hinojosa, married, according to the Roman Catholic ritual, to Don Sebastian Pancorbo, was on the threshold of forty, an age at which she had acquired the property of a robust, well-proportioned body, without crossing the line into obesity.

Her physiognomy revealed, at the first glance, a kindly soul that, if she had lived her life in a more favourable centre than the one in which it had been her fate to be born, would have attained nobility and elevated aspirations.

She was among the best-attired women in Killac and environs.

Her fingers were full of inexpensive rings; from her ears hung enormous "teething rings" of gold, circled with tiny diamonds. Her dress of coffee-coloured merino was trimmed with numerous narrow ruffles; her cashmere shawl of red and black plaid with long heavy fringe was fastened on the right side with a silver brooch in the form of an eagle.

Doña Petronila is the type of the true provincial woman, sympathetic, open-hearted, and generous; ever ready to share the sorrows of all, let them be friend or stranger; a type unknown on the Peruvian coast, where elegance in dress and more refined manners and customs do not allow a just idea of that class of women who possess hearts of gold and angel souls enshrined in a bust of clay badly modelled. Doña Petronila, carefully educated, would have been a notable person socially. In reality she was a precious jewel lost among the stones and rocks of Killac.

If, generally speaking, woman is a rough diamond and it belongs to man and education to convert her into a brilliant, to nature also is given a large share in the unfolding of the best sentiments of woman when she becomes a mother.

Doña Petronila was the mother of a youth of marked intelligence, who must have inherited the virtues of his mother, for, be it by the grace of predestination, or be it because God in His mercy had helped him to conquer in the battle between good and evil, the fact remains that he had kept himself from being contaminated by the oppressive current of depravity which exists in small towns called, with good reason, great *infiernos.*

12

MARCELA
PAYS THE
PRIEST

Marcela, on going to the priest's house accompanied by her graceful daughter Margarita and carrying the forty silver dollars, found the priest Pascual seated near the door of his office, by an old, rough pine table covered with a cloth which might have been blue in ages past. He held in his right hand a breviary with the forefinger inserted in the volume, while he mechanically recited the prayer of the day.

Marcela approached with timid step and gave the customary salute: "Hail, Mary most holy! Father," and bent down to kiss the hand of the priest, telling Margarita to do the same. The priest, fixing his eyes on the young girl, replied: "Conceived without sin!" then added: "Where did you find this young girl so pretty and plump?"

"She is my daughter, Father," replied Marcela.

"And how is it that I am not acquainted with her?" inquired Father Pascual, grabbing hold of the girl's left cheek with three fingers.

"It is because I seldom come here, for I had not paid our debt; that is why you do not remember her, Father."

"And how old is she?"

"I have counted some fourteen years since her baptism, señor padre."

"Ah, then it was not I who sprinkled her; it is hardly six years since I came. And, well, this year you will put her into the service of the church, will you not? She can begin by washing the dishes and attending to other little things."

"Father!"

"And you, lazy one, when do you begin the *mita?* Is it not already your turn?" said the priest, fixing his eyes on Marcela and getting familiar with her, patting her on the back.

"Yes, Father," said the woman trembling.

"Or, have you come to stay now?"

"Not yet, Father. I have come to pay the forty dollars for the burial of my mother-in-law, that our potato crop may be free."

"Ah, ah! So we have money, eh? Who visited your house last night?"

"No one, Father."

"No one, eh? Some deception you have practised upon your husband, and I will teach you better than to enter upon such mischief with certain people, so setting a bad example to this girl."

"Do not speak so, Father!" exclaimed the woman entreatingly, lowering her eyes and blushing, and at the same time putting forty dollars upon the table.

On seeing the money, the priest, for a moment, forgot his first idea and, dropping the breviary which he had kept under his arm, began to count and examine the money. When he had satisfied himself as to the quantity and quality of the money, and put it safely away, he turned to Marcela again and said: "Well, here are the forty dollars, and now tell me, woman, where did you get this money? Who went to your house last night?"

"Do not speak so, Father; wrong judgment coming from the lips oppresses the breast like a stone."

"Indian! Who has taught you these sayings? Speak plainly!"

"No one, Father, my soul is clean."

"And where did you get this money? You cannot deceive me. I will know all about it."

"A Christian, Father," answered Marcela, lowering her eyes and pretending to cough.

"A Christian! There is a cat in the bag, here."

"Speak, because I—wish to return you the money."

"The Señora Lucia lent it to me; but now give me the change that I may go," said Marcela, timid for having broken, by that revelation, the first command of her benefactress.

And the priest, on hearing the name of the wife of Señor Marin, said, as if stung by the viper of spite:

"Change? What change? Some other day I will give it to you." And biting his lips with repressed passion murmured, "Lucia! Lucia!"

The priest returned to his seat, taking little notice of the submissive leave-taking of Marcela and her daughter. He watched them go off, muttering bits of this and that. Perhaps he was taking up his prayers where he had left off, interrupted by the wife of Juan Yupanqui.

13
SOLD
TO ROCHINO

The return of Don Fernando to his house was the cause of rejoicing. He came triumphantly with Juan and Rosalia; he was to receive manifestations of gratitude from his wife; to taste the satisfaction of having performed a good act; to inhale the perfumed air which sweetens the hours that follow those in which one has consoled the unfortunate or dried their tears.

Lucia wept for joy. Her tears were the blessed rain that gives peace and happiness to noble hearts.

Juan knelt before the Señor Marin and bade Rosalia kiss the
hands of those who had saved her.

Don Fernando contemplated for a moment the picture before him with a tender heart, then seated himself upon the sofa,
saying to his wife: "I seldom deceive myself, my dear; I believe
that Don Sebastian is deeply wounded in his self-esteem by my
intervention in favour of these people."

"I do not doubt it, Fernando; but what can he do by way of
reprisal?" replied Lucia, passing her hand over his hair.

"A great deal, my angel; a great deal. I am truly sorry that I
have invested so much capital in this mining company with the
understanding that it would be a question of a year at the most."

"Yes, my Fernando, but remember we are on the side of right."

"I will find some way of arranging it," said Don Fernando,
when Marcela and Margarita entered full of joy and both gave
themselves up to lively transports of affection, now with Juan,
now with Rosalia, who they feared had been sold for exportation.

"Señor, señora, *Dios pagarasunqui!*" (May God repay you!) exclaimed Marcela. "O Rosa, my Rosa! Where would they have
carried you, daughter mine, if it had not been for the charity of
these angels of kindness," said the mother in tender accents.

Lucia, desirous of knowing the result of her commission, inquired of Marcela, "How did you succeed? How satisfied you
seem to be!"

Marcela, putting Rosalia to one side and assuming a respect-
ful attitude, replied; "Señor, the Father has his soul sold to
Rochino."

"And who is this Rochino?" interrupted Lucia.

It was Juan who replied, smiling: "Señora, Rochino is the
green spirit who lives in the valley of sighs which always has a
smell of brimstone; he buys souls to sell them afterwards at the
highest price in the *Manchay puito.*"

"Jesus! What a spirit; it makes me afraid!" said Lucia laughing, and turning to her husband she asked:

"Do you know, Fernando, what is the *Manchay puito?*"

"The frightful *Infierno,*" replied Don Fernando, whose curiosity was awakened by the manner in which Marcela began her
story, and in his turn he asked: "Why do you say that the priest
has sold his soul to Rochino?"

"Alas, señor! When I told the priest that I was going to pay him he began to examine me, asked who slept last night in my house, said it was some blackguard with whom I had been unfaithful to Juan."

"The priest said that to you?" interrupted Lucia, terror-stricken.

"Yes, señora, and said other things to make me confess."

"And then?"

"I had to tell him."

"What did you tell?" asked Juan with so much interest that Lucia had to laugh.

"The truth plainly."

"And what truth was that? Speak plainly," said Juan.

"That the Señora Lucia had lent me the money."

"You told him?" said the Señora Lucia angrily.

"Yes, señora, pardon my disobedience," replied Marcela with a supplicating air, "but in no other way would the priest allow me to leave his house."

"Badly done, very badly done!" said Lucia, greatly annoyed.

"This is clearer than that of the Governor, my dear, because if Don Pascual agreed to arrange it, what does it matter that he knows that you gave the money?" explained her husband.

"He said he would give the change another day," continued Marcela. "He seemed quite pleased with Margarita, said she must soon enter the service of the church."

"Margarita!" exclaimed Lucia, without trying to hide her annoyance.

"Yes, señora," replied Marcela, taking Margarita by the hand and presenting her to them.

The glance of Don Fernando rested searchingly upon the face of Margarita as he said to his wife: "Have you noticed the peculiar beauty of this girl?"

"Have I not, Fernando? From the time I first saw her I have been deeply interested in her."

"This child ought to be carefully educated," said Don Fernando, taking the hand of Margarita who, silently, as a carnation, showed her beauty and diffused the perfume of her charms.

"She is going to be our godchild, Fernando," said Lucia.

"We shall speak about that to-morrow; for to-day go and

rest calmly," said Don Fernando rising, and giving two gentle
pats on the cheeks to Margarita and Rosalia. The family of Yupanqui left, renewing their expressions of gratitude: "May God

"How old is Margarita?" inquired Don Fernando of Lucia
when they were alone.

"Her mother says she is fourteen, but her shape, her beauty,
the fire in her black eyes, everything about her indicates the tone
a woman takes on once she enters puberty."

"That is not strange, my dear, in this climate. But now we
must think of something else. You remember that we owe several visits to Doña Petronila, and I would like to go to-night, so
perhaps she will not retain a bad impression from what Don Sebastian may have told her."

"As you like, Fernando; Doña Petronila is an excellent woman.
As regards the money, I entreat you to arrange with the Governor and pay him; you know what these people are when a dollar
escapes their hands. See how the priest remained in peace after
receiving the money. Here is the remainder of the two hundred
dollars that I asked of you."

"I will take care that everything is arranged and the money
delivered."

"Fernando, how good you are! I will tell Doña Petronila so if
the opportunity offers. And, by the way, they tell me that her
son will arrive soon."

"I am very sorry, because a young man living here very soon
becomes ruined."

"Well, Fernando, I am going to change my dress, but will not
keep you waiting long."

14

THE
PLOT A s soon as Marcela had left
his house, the priest called a *pongo*
and said to him: "Run quickly to the house of Don Sebastian
and tell him that I wish to see him immediately—to come with

the friends. Then go to the house of Don Estéfano and tell him to come. Afterwards make up the fire and put on the chocolate dish, then tell Manuela and Bernarda to prepare themselves."

"Yes, Father!" and the *pongo* went out with the air of a postillion.

Don Sebastian happened to be just leaving his house, wrapped in his everlasting cape, when the messenger arrived, and after hearing the message, said to the *pongo*, "Go back home, I will tell the friends." So saying, he turned towards the house of Estéfano; nevertheless, the *pongo*, to fulfil the order of his master, went also to the house, then with his quick step returned instantly home, going directly to the kitchen to finish the second part of his duties there.

When Pancorbo entered the house of Estéfano Benites, he found him seated at a small table playing cards with the same friends who had been with him at the Governor's house.

As soon as Estéfano heard the message of the priest Pascual, he threw the cards upon the table saying: "Let us go, comrades, the church calls us!"

They all went out together, just as Don Sebastian appeared, who, saluting them, said: "I am pleased to meet you altogether; really, our priest needs us."

"Come on, then; perhaps he needs someone to help him in the *dominus vobiscum*," added Benites, and, laughing at the joke, all continued their way.

The influence exercised by the priest in these places is such that his word almost ranks as a sacred command, and such is the docility of character of the Indian that, although in the privacy of their cabins, they criticise certain acts of the priest, yet the power of superstition wielded by him overpowers all reason and makes his word the law of his followers.

The house of Benites was only three blocks from the parochial residence, so the priest had not long to wait, and at the first notice of their arrival he went to the door to receive his visitors.

"Good afternoon, gentlemen! This is what I like; people who are attentive," giving his hand to each one.

"At your service, holy Father," responded all in chorus, taking off their hats.

"Take seats; here Don Sebastian, there Don Estéfano; make yourselves comfortable, gentlemen," with a great show of hospitality.

"Thanks, we are quite comfortable. Really, Father, you are very amiable!"

"Well, gentlemen, affairs are precipitating themselves upon us, and I am obliged to trouble you," continued the priest, turning about as if seeking something.

"It is no trouble, Father," replied everyone.

"Yes, gentlemen, but we are not going to talk with our throats dry," and taking a bunch of keys he opened a cupboard and took out some bottles and glasses. Putting them on the table he said: "This is a little liquor with *anis;* it will do us no harm."

"You are very kind, Father, but really, do not trouble yourself; let the young men serve," suggested Don Sebastian, and at the word Estéfano hastened to take the bottle and began to serve the company while the priest seated himself by Don Sebastian.

"To your health, gentlemen!"

"To yours, Father," and the brimming glasses were drained.

Don Sebastian, downing his drink and spitting at the last, said: "What a comfortable little drink, really . . . the real stuff," and his opinion was echoed by all.

Raising his empty glass, Father Pascual began: "Well, children, they have humiliated me beyond measure, throwing in my face the money which the Indian Yupanqui owed me, about which we were talking the other day."

"How? What? This is insupportable, Father! Really! The same happened to-day with me," said Don Sebastian. "It is a direct attack upon Father Pascual and the Governor," broke in Estéfano. "No, no, we will not consent!"

"We must punish them, really," said Don Sebastian, tapping on the floor with the heel of his boot.

"Yes, children, it is too much to permit them to take the eyes out of our head before we are dead," continued the priest.

"Let us act at once! Tell us what we can do," said Escobedo, helping himself to another glass, saying to Estéfano in an undertone: "What luck! They left the bottle uncorked."

"I will direct the campaign!" shouted Estéfano with enthusiasm.

"If you wish I am ready also," said the Governor.

"Let us work separately," suggested the priest, accepting the glass which Escobedo offered him; and from that moment each one began to drink at their pleasure until it was necessary to open the cupboard again for a fresh supply of bottles.

The effect of the liquor soon became apparent in excited spirits and heated discourses.

Father Pascual called the *pongo* to him and said quietly: "Has the water boiled?"

"Yes, Father; and the señora has come."

"Very well. Tell her to pass into the alcove and await me there; and you bring everything ready."

The *pongo*, accustomed to that kind of service, quickly brought the cups and teapot well filled.

"Let us take a cup of tea, gentlemen," said the priest.

"So much trouble!" responded several at once.

"I will take charge of this," offered Escobedo, taking the teapot.

"Now that we are going to treat the business seriously, we have done wrong in all coming here together," said Estéfano in a tone of caution.

"That is true; we must go out separately," observed Escobedo.

"It would be well to call the sexton and explain the thing falsely," suggested the priest, swallowing his tea quickly.

"We must give a final and decisive blow, really," added Don Sebastian.

"Without missing our aim, as happened in the case of the Frenchman."

"The business is, attack and take without their getting away; Don Fernando, Doña Lucia, and . . . ."

"Kill them!"

"Bravo!"

The sound of several cups dashed upon their saucers formed an accompaniment to that criminal plot in which sentence of death was passed upon Don Fernando Marin and his wife.

The priest added: "This warning to the sexton is indispensable, so that I need not appear."

"Yes, Father. We will say that some highwaymen are planning to attack the church, and he must be ready to ring the alarm at the first notice," said Benites.

"Very well. I will take charge of the signal," volunteered Escobedo.

"It would be a good plan to spread the notice all over the town in different forms; really, we must take all precautions in regard to future investigations," observed Pancorbo.

Various comments followed, such as "I will say that they are going to rob the priest's house."

"I, that a disbanded battalion is coming."

"I will say that a band from Arequipa wish to carry off our immaculate Virgin."

"Magnificent! But the people will go to church!"

"No, señor! That is to bring them together, and afterwards we will say that the robbers have taken refuge at Don Fernando's, and . . . *cataplum!*" explained Benites.

"Yes. That is good; the rest will rush at once, because when people are excited they do not wait to reason," said Father Pascual, offering a glass to Estéfano and another to Escobedo.

"We must not forget to compromise the judge. I will go there and deceive him."

"Really, that cannot be overlooked."

"The judge has a little love nest where he goes to see La Quiquijaneña. I will go there and give him some trumped-up explanation," offered Benites.

"Now let us go."

"Be prudent, children," said the priest warningly, as they retired quietly, going in different directions.

Pascual and the Governor remained talking privately, not forgetting to refresh themselves with the liquor that remained.

"That boy Benites is worth money! Audacious and careful," observed the priest.

"True, Father. That matter of the judge we were forgetting."

"It is true that the young men of to-day know a great deal."

"And he is sure to find him over there with La Quiquijaneña. Really, what a spicy little number she is! It is my belief that you, too, Father, are no stranger to those parts of town, really," said Don Sebastian roguishly, to which the other replied laughing: "Why, Governor!" and slapped him on the back.

"Good-night, Father, it is time to retire, and really the night is cold."

"Take a sleeping draught," said Don Pascual, filling two glasses and passing one to Don Sebastian.

Half an hour later, in the saloons and all places where drink abounded, might be heard the sound of revelry and disputes, and dancing guided by the silvery guitar.

And the victims designed for the sacrifice, with peace in their souls and felicity in their loving hearts, went at that same hour to the house of Don Sebastian, their secret enemy, to visit his wife.

15

THE ASSAULT

The sun of happiness and joy illuminated the house of Doña Petronila with its purest rays. Doña Petronila was a happy mother, because she had folded in her arms, after a long absence, her son Manuel; the dream of her sleeping hours, the comfort of her sad days, the son of her heart.

Manuel, who went away from Killac a boy, had returned grown into a noble man, serious and thoughtful, for he had made the very best of his student life in Lima.

Manuel was found seated at his mother's side, her hands clasped in his as he gazed upon her with the tenderest satisfaction, while they conversed confidentially on family matters.

Don Fernando and Doña Lucia appeared at the door. On seeing them, mother and son rose to their feet to receive their visitors.

"Señora Lucia, Señor Marin, this is my son who went away a little lad. You will hardly recognize him; he has just arrived after an absence of seven years. Please take seats," indicating the sofa.

"What a pleasant young man is your son, Doña Petronila," observed Lucia when all were seated.

Manuel was a youth of twenty summers, of medium height, pleasant countenance, and sonorous but sweet voice that at once won the sympathy and attention of his hearers. Above his fine, rosy lips was a very black moustache, and his large eyes stood out all the more for the circles under them. His way with words and his cultivated bearing completed the portrait of an interesting young man.

"Have you chosen a profession?" asked Don Fernando, addressing Manuel.

"Yes, Señor Marin, I am studying law and am in the second year. I expect to be a lawyer if fortune favours me," replied Manuel modestly.

"I congratulate you, my friend. The vast field of jurisprudence offers charms to an intelligent person."

"Any other profession, also, señor, if you consecrate to it your will and your love," responded Manuel.

At this moment they heard the report of firearms which frightened the ladies and excited the men.

Lucia took her husband's arm quickly, saying: "Come, come, Fernando, let us go."

"Yes, yes, señora, go quickly and secure well the entrance to your house," said Doña Petronila confusedly.

"But what can it be?" asked Manuel.

"It is something unusual here," observed Don Fernando. And Lucia exclaimed, "It may be robbers!"

"Let us go," said Don Fernando, offering his arm to his wife. But Manuel interposed, asking that he might be permitted to accompany the señora and giving her his arm.

The three went away together.

Doña Petronila said to herself: "My mother's heart cannot remain calm while my Manuel is out of the house," and she followed the group at a little distance with cautious steps.

Manuel, who from the first had been strongly drawn towards the Señor and Señora Marin, remarked: "Señora, I, who on arriving at Killac, thought I should die of loneliness, have found it brightened and cheered by the presence of yourself and of your husband."

"Thanks, sir. You have well learned the gallant phrases of the city," replied Lucia smiling.

"No, señora! My words are wanting in the gallantry of mere form. Apart from yourselves and my mother, with whom can I associate here? This afternoon I have become acquainted with some of the neighbours of the town, and it has given me sorrow and compassion."

"That is quite true, Don Manuel, but you have your parents and will have us for friends."

"Yes, Don Manuel; for a person who comes from the city, it is very lonely. You are right," said Don Fernando.

"Only I am afraid we shall not remain here very long, because I think Fernando's business will soon be arranged," answered Lucia.

"So much the worse for us if I had to prolong my stay here, which I expect now will only be about six months," said Manuel.

Don Fernando stepped forward to open the street door, having arrived at their house.

"Come in and rest, Manuel," said Lucia.

"No thank-you, señora. My mother will be anxious about me if I tarry and I wish to save her all anxiety," replied Manuel.

"Our house is yours, friend," offered Don Fernando.

"Thanks. I appreciate your kindness, and will give myself the pleasure of a visit very soon. Good-night!" replied Manuel, shaking hands with his friends and disappearing in the dark streets of Killac, where here and there the odd drunk wandered about.

Don Fernando and Lucia took some precautions about securing the house, but seeing that all seemed tranquil retired to sleep.

The surface of a crystalline lake, wherein is reflected the image of passing birds, is not so placid as the sleep with which

they were soothed by the Angel of Love beating his ivory wings
over the brows of Lucia and Fernando. Their hearts, linked together in peace, throbbed happily in unison.

But this sleep was not like the eternal stupor of matter. The
spirit, which does not sleep, struggled with the power of presen-
timent; that mysterious warning voice of good souls shook the
sensitive organism of Lucia and awoke her, inspiring her with
hesitation, fear, doubt, all that complicated array of sensations
which comes to one during nights of sleeplessness. Lucia felt
those nervous tremblings which indicated to her some unknown
danger and her thoughts flew to the memory of those midnight
sounds that, like wings brushing past or a door creaking, first inspire fear and then the memory of loved ones, whether far away
or giving one an affectionate hug. She waited and watched. The
old town clock gave the twelve strokes that mark the midnight
hour; the next moment vibrated on the midnight air the heavy
tones of the church bell. Its brazen voice did not invite to quiet
prayer and rest of soul; it called the neighbours to assault and
battle, according to the agreement between Estéfano and the
sexton who waited in the tower. And like the hail which the
black clouds pour upon the defenceless earth, stones and balls
began to rain down upon the undefended home of Fernando
Marin.

A thousand shadows crossed and recrossed the yard and
street in different directions, and a deafening roar went up like a
gigantic wave which the tempest raises on the bosom of the angry sea to break with a voice of thunder on the rocky coast. The
mob was terrifying. The voices of command, hoarse and contradictory, could be heard above the noise of stones and shot and
balls.

"Foreigners!" "Robbers! *"Suhua! Suhua!* (Thieves!)" "Meddlers!"
came cries from all sides.

"Death to them!" *"Huañuchly!* (Kill them!)" a thousand voices
repeated. And the clanging tones of the alarm bell were the only
response to all these wild cries.

Lucia and Fernando abandoned their peaceful bed, clad only
in their scanty night robes and the little they could catch up in

passing, to fly from or fall into the hands of their implacable enemies, to suffer a cruel death in the midst of that multitude,
drunk with alcohol and wrath.

16
HOPE
RENEWED

Juan Yupanqui and Marcela, who, after these events, left Lucia's house, arrived home with Margarita and Rosalia, those
two laughing stars in their cabin, whose destinies bore the mark
God places on all who are predestined in the map of society's
evolution.

The brain of Juan Yupanqui no longer harbored the criminal
thoughts of the night before. He would no longer stand on the
dark threshold of suicide, an act that plunges into mourning the
hearts of those left behind and kills the hopes of those who
believe.

God sent Lucia so that Juan would trust again in Providence;
his faith had been torn from his heart by Father Pascual, the
Governor, and the debt collector or *cacique*—the terrifying trinity summed up in a single injustice.

Juan believed again in good; he was rehabilitated; and he was
going to throw himself into the business of living with fresh
vigor, to show his eternal gratitude to his benefactors.

Marcela would not, after all, be the widow of a suicide, of a
deserter from life, whose cadaver, buried on a river bank or by
the side of some solitary road, would not bring peace, sighs, or
tears from his loved ones.

Sitting in their cabin, Juan said to his wife:

"Let us offer up our praise, and from this moment I swear to
you I will dedicate my efforts and my life to our protectors."

"Juanuco! Did I not tell you? And I, too, will serve them until I'm old."

"Me, too, Mama," added Margarita.

After explaining to Rosalia that those wicked men would

have taken her away if it had not been for the supplications of
Wiracocha Fernando and Doña Lucia of the "big house," all
four knelt, and with hands raised to heaven, offered the beautiful prayers of blessing and thanksgiving.

"Now get the fire going," said Juan to Marcela.

"We will roast some potatoes, and here is some garlic,"
replied Marcela, taking out some maize husks wrapped up and
tied with wool yarn.

"Tomorrow let us kill a chicken, Marcela; I am as happy as
can be, and our *compadre* will surely lend us a few pesos," said
Juan contentedly.

"This is how I like to see you, *tata*. Or we can ask for the
change the priest still has," replied the woman, setting down
near her husband two glazed earthenware dishes.

"What change? For how much?" said Yupanqui.

"How lovely our Margarita will be when she becomes the
goddaughter of Señora Marin, will she not?" said the woman,
changing the topic.

"You can count on that. She will dress her up in the clothes
they wear."

"But my heart aches when I remember that she will not look
at us anymore the way she does now, when Margarita becomes a
young lady," said Marcela, sighing and coming over to add a log
to the fire.

"Why do you think that? Señora Lucia will teach her to respect us," the Indian responded.

"Bless her! *Pachamama!* (Blessed lady!)" said Marcela raptly.

"Mama, when Señora Lucia becomes any godmother, will I
go live with her?" asked Margarita.

"Yes, daughter," answered the mother.

"What about you, and my Juan and Rosalia?" asked Margarita insistently.

"We will come see you every day," answered Marcela without
interrupting her cooking; while Juan was cuddling Rosalia on
his lap, he said to his wife:

"Looks like you let something slip out."

"That is what it looks like," said Marcela, turning the potatoes; but Margarita asked again:

"And will you bring me the berries and the sparrows' nests?"

"Yes, we will bring you all that if you learn to sew and knit the beautiful needlework Señora Lucia knows how to do," answered Marcela, while she took the potatoes out and placed them in the dishes over by her husband.

The supper was tasty and frugal; but Rosalia's prayer reached up to heaven, bringing refreshing sleep to the family of Juan Yupanqui, resting without nagging doubts in the humble bed of satisfaction.

A deep yawn from Juan let Marcela know that her husband was completely asleep and that their daughters had followed his example, so that the cabin remained in absolute silence.

And while the shades of Quietude dwell here, let us see what is happening in the parochial house.

17

EVIL

DEEDS A black shadow, impatient and excited, paced from one end of

the dark room to the other, for the priest had not the courage to light the lamp of linseed oil, then in use, or the tallow candle of home manufacture. Crime always loves the darkness of night.

Nearly in front of a small window, the woodwork of which was painted yellow, was placed an old *catre*, or folding bed, the sides made of precious Zumbaillo wood and covered with some ancient silk damask curtains. The wide comfortable bed, with its curious covering of a patchwork quilt made of a thousand samples of Cashmere of divers colours ingeniously combined by some busy woman or the hand of some holy sister of the city, was half open and in a certain degree of disorder.

By the side of the bed, seated upon a wooden bench, and leaning a little on the pillows, was a woman who had been secretly admitted by the *pongo* early in the evening.

Father Pascual was waiting for the result of the plans formed

by him—waiting in darkness that no suspicion might fall on
him by a light being seen at that hour of the night. Once in a
while he would pause with his ear at a crack in the window.

"What is the matter with you, man of God? I have never seen
you so restless as you are tonight!" the woman ventured to say.

"Did you not hear that shot?" stammered the priest, for the
liquor was taking effect, and impeded him from speaking
clearly.

"That shot? But that was hours ago, and everything is tranquil now," argued the woman.

"They might rob the church; bad news was brought me this
afternoon by the neighbours," said the priest, with the idea of
deceiving the woman, for the thought of appearing innocent
still filled his brain.

"Robbers in Killac, robbers for the church! Ha, ha!" exclaimed the woman loudly.

"Hush, woman of my sins!" hissed the priest with manifest
anger, stamping on the floor with his foot.

"But, man, come over here; lie down a moment."

"Hush, you demon!" interrupted Father Pascual.

"Do not be so clumsy this time, after . . . how clumsy you
were," replied the woman as if trying to pick a fight.

And the priest had no other way to keep her from speaking
aloud, in an accusing voice, than to go to her and lie down beside her, taking out of his pocket a silk handkerchief, which she
tied around his head.

An owl passed that night over the roof of the parochial
house, flapping his dark wings and proclaiming ill fortune in
that dismal croak which is the terror of simple-minded people.

Don Sebastian had not returned home.

Doña Petronila summoned two servants to send in search of
her husband, to accompany him home; but Manuel said, taking
his hat and cane: "I will go, Mother."

"By no means; I will not consent. Alas, my son! I do not
know what my heart warns me of. That shot, the prolonged absence of your father; the comings and goings of Estéfano—all
keep me preoccupied," said Doña Petronila mournfully.

But Manuel, inspired by the nobleness of his sentiments, and perhaps by a double desire, replied: "For that same reason I should go in search of Don Sebastian and take him away from danger or from foolish engagements."

"It would be useless, my son; you do not understand his obstinate disposition. O! I beg you, Manuel, I implore you, to remember that your duty commands you to take care of me; I am your mother; do not leave me alone; in God's name I ask it!"

"Very well, I will not go, Mother," replied Manuel, taking off his hat.

"In that case perhaps I can go to sleep," said his mother, with a sigh of relief.

"Go to bed, Mother, the night is cold and it is late."

"Go to your room, my son. Good-night!" said Doña Petronila, looking at her son with much satisfaction.

18
THE
INDIAN'S
GRATEFULNESS

At the first tones of the bell and the report of the firearms, the servants of Don Fernando fled in terror, for they understood that the point of attack was their master's house.

Don Fernando prepared for defence, and went to take down a rifle well supplied with ammunition; but Lucia interposed supplicatingly, repeating in anguish: "No, Fernando mine, no! Save yourself; save me; let us save ourselves."

"But what shall I do, my dear? There is no remedy. We shall die defenceless," he replied, trying to calm his wife.

"Let us flee, Fernando."

"Where to, my dear Lucia? The entrance to the house is already gained," said he, putting a box of cartridges into the pocket of his trousers.

The shouts were repeated in the streets, each time more terrible and implacable.

"Highwaymen!" "Foreigners!" "To the death!" were some of
the words that rose above the wild roar of this whirlwind of
passion, a drunken mob.

Suddenly a new voice was heard, fresh and clear; free from
the effects of alcohol which, with all the confidence and serenity
of courage, said: "Leave this place, you miserable men! No one
shall be assassinated here!"

And another voice, supporting the first, saying: "We have
been deceived. There are no such robbers!"

"Come to this side, all honest men!" shouted imperatively
the first voice.

At that moment a woman came up, provided with a lantern
containing a tallow candle which gave a faint light. The shots
and the clanging of the bell ceased. People began to disperse in
different directions, and the reaction of the mob was complete.

The entrance to the house of Don Fernando was totally destroyed and great piles of stones lay beside the doors, which
were entirely demolished.

"Bring that lantern here!" cried a man, opening a passage
through the remaining groups of men. By the faint light shed by
the lantern Manuel recognised his mother.

"Mother! You here?" he exclaimed in surprise.

"My son, here I am at your side," replied Doña Petronila, her
face full of horror.

She gave the lantern to her son and together they began to
look for the dead and wounded.

The first body they found was that of an Indian, and at his
feet was a woman bathed in blood and tears, shrieking in des-
peration: "Ay! Ay! They have killed my husband, and they will
have murdered also my protectors!"

At the sound of the first shot, Juan and Marcela had rushed
over to help protect the house of Don Fernando. Juan fell
pierced by a ball which passed through his right lung, broke the
second rib as it came out, and grazed his liver. Marcela had a
wound in the shoulder from which the blood was streaming.
Near them lay the bodies of three defenceless Indians.

"Mother!" called Manuel, "This Indian woman will die in a
few minutes if she does not have help immediately."

"Let us take her away from here and bring the doctor to see her," replied Doña Petronila.

"Here, some men!" shouted Manuel, and several men presented themselves offering to carry Marcela.

Manuel, the intrepid youth who had defied the drunken populace, opened a passage, and restrained the mob, saying himself as he saw the solicitude of all to gather up the dead and attend to the wounded: "The assault was the fruit of an error more worthy of pardon than punishment."

Several men raised Marcela, now almost helpless, to take her where she could be treated.

"Slowly, carefully," said Doña Petronila.

"Ay! Ay! Where do you take me?" asked Marcela, covering her wound with one hand; then she burst out: "My daughters! Rosa! Margarita!"

"What has become of Don Fernando and Doña Lucia?" asked Manuel with growing interest; and at that moment the light of a new day began to flicker faintly on the faces of the innocent victims and of the guilty instigators of the foul crime.

19

MELITONA
GLEANING
NEWS

Someone else besides Manuel was interested in knowing what fate had befallen the family of Señor Marin. And that was the priest Pascual, who performed prodigies of invention, in order to smooth over explanations with Doña Melitona, the woman who had accompanied him that fearful night.

As soon as the bell was silent and the shots had ceased, Pascual said to himself: "By this time some result has been obtained." Turning to Melitona and endeavouring to speak quietly, he said: "The tumult seems to be finished, eh?"

"Yes. It seems to have passed away, but what a fright I have had!" said Melitona.

"And I not less, from the moment I heard the first shot, believing that they were attacking the church, and you were so unbelieving."

"Happily we soon persuaded ourselves that it was somewhere else. And what if I had permitted you to go out?"

"Heaven protect me! You did well, Melitona, in keeping me here."

"And what will have been the trouble?" asked the woman innocently.

"O! Political matters. Thanks to God that I did not go out. Thanks, thanks," repeated the priest, burning with a desire to know the result of the attack but not daring to let his anxiety be known.

As soon as the day began to break and people were heard passing in the streets, he said to the woman: "Melitona! You, who are a woman, must be full of curiosity; go and find out what really occurred last night. It seems to me it must have been over in the direction of the house of Señor Marin. I must prepare for celebrating mass."

"I will go at once," replied Melitona, quite contented with her commission.

She crossed herself three times, put on her mantle of brown cashmere with a black border, and went out.

The first persons she met gave her an account of the assault on the house of Don Fernando Marin; but desirous of carrying to the parochial house news of what she had seen with her own eyes, she introduced herself into the very scene of the conflict.

"Jesus! What temerity! What heretics can have done this? Poor Señor Marin! Poor Señora Lucia! See, everything destroyed," she said, walking about amongst the ruins before the door.

Don Fernando and Doña Lucia, safe and sound, were in the office surrounded by a group of anxious and indignant people. Manuel, with all the indignation of his pure heart and the fire of youth, exclaimed: "Such iniquity is inconceivable, Don Fernando. These are an ignorant and barbarous people, and your salvation is nothing short of a miracle. Tell us how you saved yourselves."

"The miracle is Lucia's," responded Don Fernando dryly, tying his cravat, which, in the confusion, had become loose, and pacing back and forth through the room.

"Señora Lucia," said Manuel, turning towards the sofa where that lady reclined, the deepest emotion depicted on her countenance.

Don Fernando, as if following the course of his thoughts, continued: "What horror! Many know what it is to awake in the night in the midst of tumult and confusion, strife and bloodshed, because the country witnesses and allows these uprisings and civil conflicts, which, now in one name now in another, bring terror and grief, be it in the dawn of revolution or in the strongholds resisting an attack, but few understand what it is to awake from tranquil, happy sleep, amid the leaden hail and the shouts of cut-throats coming from the walls of their own dwelling."

"Enough, Don Fernando, enough!" cried several voices in chorus.

"What an atrocity!" added Manuel.

Don Fernando, answering Manuel's first question, which at first had been unheeded in the natural tumult of thoughts, said: "I was resolved, Don Manuel, to sacrifice myself and fight to the last, but the tears of my good wife made me think of saving myself in order to save her also. We both fled by the left side of the house and took refuge behind a stone wall just in front of the place attacked. From there we witnessed the assault upon our house, the massacre of Juan and Marcela, your own heroism and the maternal abnegation of Doña Petronila."

"Poor Juan! Poor Marcela! Now that misfortune has made us sisters, my tenderest solicitude will be for her and her daughters," said Lucia sighing sadly.

"Yes. Margarita and Rosalia, these poor doves without a nest, shall find from to-day the protection of a father in this house," affirmed Don Fernando.

"Let Marcela be brought here and attended to carefully," said Lucia tenderly, and, turning to Manuel, added: "Manuel, I entreat you in the name of friendship to take charge of this." To which Manuel responded with all the vehemence of youth:

"I go this moment, señora. You, good angel, will staunch the wounds of the widow, and we, Don Fernando, will bring to account those who are culpable."

On uttering these last words a mortal paleness overspread his countenance. The name of Don Sebastian crossed his mind; Sebastian, the husband of his mother, the man to whom he gave the name of "father"!

Taking his hat mechanically, he saluted and went out quickly, passing on the way Doña Melitona, who had listened from the door without losing a word.

Don Fernando seated himself beside his wife, on the sofa, and Melitona, thinking she had gleaned sufficient news, returned to inform the priest, who was impatiently awaiting her arrival, "It is time to celebrate Mass!"

Melitona entered, and, taking off her mantle, began: "I bring everything hot, Father."

"Yes, Melitona? And how was it?"

"They say that Don Fernando had some business, I do not know what, with some wool buyers, and Don Sebastian put in his hand in favour of I do not know whom, and from that came the dispute, and then a quarrel; and someone else thought they were robbers and rang the bells," related Melitona with numerous gestures and noddings of the head.

"It was private business, then; a good beating will I give the sexton and he will not be quite so quick with his bells another time," replied the priest.

"That is what they say, Father; but Don Sebastian's son, a young man recently arrived, was at the house of Don Fernando and very much at home he seemed to be. He says he will have the guilty ones punished."

"He said that?" asked the priest, biting his lips, and added to himself: "Who lives longest knows most."

And the bells began to ring calling the people to mass.

20
THE
BURIAL
OF JUAN

The entrance of Marcela, who was brought on a wooden stretcher—wounded, widowed, followed by her two orphan daughters—to the same house out of which she had gone only the day before, contented and happy, impressed Lucia so deeply that she could not restrain her tears, and she went weeping to receive Marcela. After seeing her comfortably installed in a neat room, she took Rosalia in her arms and caressed Margarita as she said to them both: "Poor precious daughters."

Seating herself by the side of Marcela, she said tenderly: "O my dear, how much resignation you need! I implore you to be calm and have patience."

"Señora, do you not fear to protect us?" asked the Indian woman faintly with a languid glance.

But Lucia, without answering this question, continued: "How weak you are," and, turning to two servants near the door, ordered them to prepare some chicken broth and toasted bread and beaten egg, and to give her every care.

The countenance of Marcela revealed her terrible suffering, but the words of Lucia seemed to give her relief and strength. So great was the influence of that kind-hearted woman over her that, although the doctor had declared that her wound was mortal and the end would come soon, because the bullet was lodged in the shoulderblade, after having pierced the left shoulder, yet Marcela kept up her courage. So two days passed, giving at times a faint hope of saving the sick woman.

As Don Fernando entered one afternoon, Lucia asked with great interest: "Fernando, what about the remains of Juan?"

"I have had them taken to the cemetery with all the honours that I could give, paying all expenses myself. I had them put in a provisional grave."

"And why provisional?"

"Because it is probable that the judge will have a new examination made, doubting whether my report is correct," replied Don Fernando, taking a paper out of his pocket.

"And what does this certificate say?" asked Lucia.

Don Fernando read: "Juan Yupanqui was killed instantly by the action of a projectile thrown from a certain height which, fracturing the right scapula, followed an oblique path through both lungs, destroying the great arteries of the mediastinum."

"Will this report assist in the discovery of the perpetrator of the deed?"

"Alas, my dear, we have very little hope of accomplishing anything," replied her husband.

"And Father Pascual, what does he say?"

"Ugh! He had no more hesitancy in saying the Responses over the tomb of Juan Yupanqui than I had in placing the humble wooden cross at his grave."

"Can he be ignorant of the details of the assault upon our house?"

"He ignorant! What an idea! I believe him implicated in the plot."

"And the judge?"

"The judge and the authorities have taken some measures, such as to store away the stones piled up at our door as evidence of the assault," replied Don Fernando laughing; but immediately a look of sorrow overspread his countenance, which indicated the deep deception he had undergone.

Perhaps all these doings had caused a feeling of scepticism to spring up in that noble, just heart.

Conversing thus they passed down the hall to Lucia's room where they seated themselves, Lucia on the sofa and Don Fernando in an arm chair.

"My dear, if there is a little *chicha* with rice, will you give me a glass?"

"In a moment, dear," said Lucia, springing up and passing from the room, returning quickly with a thick brew sprinkled with cinnamon, a tempting-looking beverage, which she presented to her husband.

Don Fernando drank it eagerly, put the glass upon the table, wiped his mouth with a perfumed handkerchief, and turning to his wife said: "What a comforting drink, my dear. I do not know how it is that people prefer the beer of the country to this drink. But, returning to poor Juan, my dear, do you know that the poor Indian has awakened in me still greater interest since his death? They say that the Indians are ungrateful; Juan Yupanqui has died in shewing his gratitude."

"For me," replied Lucia, "they have not entirely extinguished in Peru that race with principles of rectitude and nobleness that characterized the founders of the empire conquered by Pizarro. Another thing is that all the people who consider themselves of high rank here have put the Indian in the same sphere as the beasts."

"There is something more, dear," said Don Fernando. "It is proven that the Indians' diet has caused their cerebral functions to degenerate. As you have no doubt noticed, these disinherited beings scarcely ever eat meat, and the advances of modern science have proven to us that cerebral activity is in direct relation to its nutritional sources. With the Indian condemned to an extremely limited vegetable diet, living on turnip greens, boiled beans, and quinoa leaves, with no albuminoids or organic salts, his brain has no source from which to draw phosphates and lecithin for psychic effort; it only serves to fatten the brain, which plunges him into the depths of cognitive darkness, making him live at the same level as his work animals."

"I believe as you do, Fernando dear, and congratulate you on your fine dissertation, even though I don't understand it, but if it were put into English, it would be good for a degree of DOCTOR at any University in the world," said Lucia laughing.

"You are teasing me! I see all it earns me here is your laughter," said Don Fernando, turning slightly red, because his wife's words made him realise he had been expounding a great deal of scientific prose, perhaps pedantic or out of place.

"No, dear, I am not making fun of you, it is just that it seems so strange to be making these formal pronouncements over the grave of an Indian as exceptional as Juan was."

"In my opinion Juan was not an uncommon specimen of his race. If the dawn should ever break of the true autonomy of the

Indian, we shall witness the regenerating evolution of a race to-
day oppressed and humiliated," replied Don Fernando.

"I do not contradict you, Fernando. But, talking about the dead we are forgetting the living. I will go to see how Marcela is getting on."

21
MANUEL
AND HIS
MOTHER

Manuel did not give himself an hour's rest from the time the terrible events were initiated which moved all Killac.

As soon as he had seen Marcela taken to the house of Lucia, he devoted himself to the work of prudent investigation, employing in it all the sagacity he had learned in his college experience.

Therefore, he avoided an immediate explanation with Don Sebastian. He also remained away from the house of Señor Marin.

One morning, on returning home, taciturn and moody, he found his mother occupied in preparing some fish for the oven.

On seeing her son Doña Petronila said: "Manuel, do you remember how you used to like this kind of fish baked in the oven? For that reason I am preparing them myself."

"Thank you, Mother. Send that to the oven, and listen to me in your room," said Manuel, to whose sad heart this tender thoughtfulness of his mother was a healing balsam. He went to his mother's room, saying to himself: "Blessed be mothers! He who has not felt the caresses and received the kiss of a mother does not know what it is to love."

Entering the room he drew a chair to the table, threw himself down heavily, and, resting his elbows on the table, let his head fall upon his hands in a meditative manner. What combinations he had made! All the threads taken in the investigations practised among his associates led him to see the true authors of the armed assault on the house of Don Fernando Marin, and among them stood boldly out the figures of Don Sebastian, the priest Pascual, and Estéfano Benites!

Doña Petronila came in and gave him a pat on the shoulder, saying: "You have been sleeping, Manuel."

Manuel, letting his arms fall, fixed his eyes on his mother with a loving expression and, rising to his feet, said: "No, Mother, not at all; the restless spirit still keeps vigil. Sit down; let us talk a while." Drawing another chair beside his own, he offered it to his mother.

"No, my son, I will sit here, on this bench; I am more comfortable here," replied Doña Petronila, seating herself on a low seat covered with a piece of carpet.

"I can guess about what you are going to speak. What things have happened; until now my soul has hardly returned to its body; I am always seeing the faces of those dead Indians, bathed in blood and covered with dirt!"

"Ah, Mother! With what fatal star have I returned to witness such tragic events, but lamentations are useless; let us have brave hearts and perhaps we can remedy things somewhat, and try to save Don Sebastian," replied Manuel.

"Oh, my son! Why should I not tell you all? Ever since they made your father Governor he has become another person. I can do nothing with him anymore."

"Yes, I know, Mother; I have understood it all from the moment I came home."

"Speak to him then. He will listen to you."

"I fear not. If I were truly his son, the voice of paternal love would speak in him—but—you know—"

"Why do you bring those things up now?" queried his mother shortly.

"Pardon me, Mother. But now let us go to the root of the matter. You must help me; but with love; without bitter words or hard charges. Nothing of that; we must try to get him to leave the governorship; and for the rest I will take the results upon my shoulders. I have it all thought out. Now I must go and see the mischief-working priest."

"Do not talk in that way of a priest; the ex-communicated person is ruined."

"Mother, the man who prostitutes his ministry merits contempt. But let us not talk of him. We must work for Don Sebastian. Go to his room; try to speak to him and prepare his mind to receive me afterwards."

"Now, at once?" she asked.

"Yes, Mother. There is no time to lose."

Doña Petronila went out slowly. On reaching the door of Don Sebastian's room she waited a moment outside, crossed herself, then entered.

Manuel remained in his mother's room walking up and down, thinking out his plans, because his interview with Don Sebastian would necessarily be rather hard for him.

As he paced about, his eye was suddenly caught by an earthenware vase on a stand in the corner, which so fascinated him that he examined it more closely and said:

"This must be a very important *huaco*; the clay is made of such fine earth . . . and these designs, the skill that went into them; and how well the potter made the *lliclla* (cape) of this *ccoya* (great lady) and the shadows from the billowing cape of this Indian, who must be the *cacique* of his tribe."

At last Doña Petronila returned joyfully. "Manuel, Don Sebastian seems to be in good humour now," she said.

"What did you say to him about the matter?"

"I only said that it would be better for him to leave the governorship, because trouble was sure to come from the discovery, and seizing of the actors in the work of the other night."

"You did not tell him, Mother, that he was pointed out as a participant?"

"Why should I tell him that? He would have danced with rage; I did not dare."

"But what did he reply at last?"

"'I know what I shall do,' he said; so go now and see him, my son."

Manuel kissed his mother's brow and went to the room of Sebastian Pancorbo, Governor of Killac.

22
THE
INSTIGATORS
INTERVIEWED

Don Sebastian was reclining in an arm chair wrapped in a plush *poncho*, his head tied up, with a red handkerchief, with the knot and ends in front. He was visibly preoccupied.

"Good morning, sir!" said Manuel on entering.

"Good morning! Where do you come from, Manuel? Really, from the time you came I have not seen you more than three times," said Don Sebastian, striving to hide his preoccupation.

"The fault is not mine, señor; you have not been at home."

"Really, these friends; the duties which I have to perform—one does not belong to himself," said the Governor, and, as if seeking some way of making his conduct appear sincere, added: "The fact is the other night, really, I was in danger, without power to restrain the disorder; but what can be done without an armed force? You acted very well, Manuel. Really, but this Don Fernando is to blame for it all."

"I have come to speak to you seriously, Don Sebastian, about what occurred the other night. I cannot remain with my arms crossed when I know that you are accused."

"I!" exclaimed Don Sebastian, jumping up.

"Yes, señor, you."

"And who is it accuses me, who? Really, I would like to know him."

"Do not excite yourself, señor; be calm, and let us speak as between father and son. Here no one hears us," replied Manuel, biting his lips.

"And you, what do you say? Speak! Really, I like the idea!"

"From all the investigations I have made, the results are, that the priest Pascual, you, and Estéfano Benites have plotted and directed this thing against Don Fernando because of the return of money that was assessed and for burial fees."

Don Sebastian kept changing colour at each word Manuel

spoke until, at the last, entirely pallid, and a prey to a nervous trembling, which he strove in vain to overcome, he said: "They say that? Really, then, we have been sold."

"It was not yourselves alone. Other individuals belonged to the conspiracy, and plots that are made among many and among the wine cups do not carry the seal of secrecy," replied Manuel calmly.

"It must be Escobedo. Really, this youth seemed to me a bad one."

"It has been someone, Don Sebastian, but this is not the time for conjectures but to put yourself in safety."

"And what is your idea, my son?"

"That you would leave the governorship immediately."

"Oh no, not that, really; I cease to be an authority in the town where I was born? No, no, do not propose such a thing to me, Manuel."

"But you will have to do it, or they will take it from you, and I ask and advise you to do it soon. You have been carried along by the current. The principal author is the priest. I will have an understanding with him. You will sign your resignation, Don Sebastian. From childhood, I have given you the name of father; everyone believes me to be your son, and you cannot doubt my interest nor despise my advice. I do it all for love to my mother, from gratitude to you," said Manuel, exhausting his arsenal of provision and wiping his brow moistened with the dew of a discussion in which he had to mention his paternity unknown to society.

Don Sebastian was moved; he embraced Manuel saying to him: "Do as you please, really. Just do not leave out the priest."

"Everything will be arranged in the best way possible for you, señor; and later we will go to see Don Fernando together, because it is better that you and he should be on good terms. Now I am going to see the priest Pascual."

When alone, Don Sebastian repeated between his teeth: "Escobedo or Benites!"

At that time Father Pascual was calmly taking his lunch, with his two cats—one black, the other white and yellow—at his side; a woolly dog slept with his head between his fore paws, stretched full length on the threshold of the room; the *pongo* with folded arms, in a humble attitude, stood near the dog awaiting his master's orders.

Hearing footsteps and seeing Manuel coming, the priest took up a soup plate and covered with it another plate on which was a young pigeon prepared after the native fashion, with two sliced tomatoes upon the wings and a sprig of parsley in its beak.

"Reverend Father," said Manuel on entering, raising his hat politely.

"Manuel, to what happy chance do I owe the pleasure of seeing you here?" was the greeting of the priest.

"The reason of my coming cannot be unknown to you, señor," replied Manuel dryly. He had gone prepared to use no compliments with the priest Pascual.

"Young man, you surprise me," said Pascual, changing his tone; and taking up a fork absently from the table, he seemed absorbed in contemplating it.

Manuel, who had remained standing, took the seat nearest to him and continued: "Without preamble, señor priest, the assault which the night before last covered the town with shame and mourning is your work."

"What do you say? Insolent boy!" said the priest, moving about in his seat, surprised at hearing for the first time such language from an equal and in an accusing tone.

"I do not qualify my words, señor priest; remember that it is not the robe that gives respect to a man, but the man who dignifies the habit which covers good as well as unworthy ministers," replied Manuel.

"And what proof have you of the truth of such an accusation?"

"All that a man needs to accuse another man," replied the young man plainly.

"And if instead of me you should meet another person before whom you would have to hang down your head ashamed?" asked the priest, throwing the fork, which he had retained in his hand, upon the table, thinking he had given a decisive blow. But Manuel, without losing his serenity in the least, responded very quietly: "The person to whom you allude, señor, has been your unhappy tool, as the others have been."

"What do you say, young man?" exclaimed the priest, angrily,

into whose mind came the thought "Can Pancorbo have revealed anything?"

"What you have heard, señor Pascual," replied Manuel. "Let
us make our conversation short."

"The shortest way will be for you to take your leave," replied
the priest furiously.

"Before I have accomplished my purpose? Do not expect it,
señor."

"And what is it you desire?" inquired the priest, changing his
tone and striving to keep his anger.

"I desire that you and Don Sebastian should repair the damage you have done, as much as possible, before the judge re-
quires it of the delinquents."

"Holy heavens! What do I hear? Don Sebastian, weak and ef-
feminate, has sold us!" exclaimed the priest, wholly conquered
by Manuel when he mentioned his father. But like a man seeking a new line of defence he continued: "Would you be such an
unnatural son as to accuse your father?"

"Of course not, since I am seeking a reparation, prudent and
deliberate, to minimise the fault which by some means must be
found, since our religious beliefs teach us that without previous
remission of sin we shall not find the door of heaven open."

"Aha! And is that what your professors have taught you,
so you may avoid accusing your father?" inquired the priest
ironically.

"More still, señor priest. They have taught me that without
rectitude of action there can be neither citizen, nor country, nor
family; and I repeat that I do not accuse Don Sebastian; I seek
satisfaction to minimise his wrongdoing," continued the young
man, when suddenly there appeared at the door a servant from
the house of Don Fernando, screaming frantically:

"Señor, señor, help for a dying person!!"

"Go, señor priest. Fulfil the duties of your office and afterwards we will talk," said Manuel, taking leave.

The priest took up his hat, and looking after Manuel, said
contemptuously, "Bah! What a mason!"

Uncovering the plate he had put by, and smelling the con-
tents, he murmured in an undertone: "The pigeon is cold; I will
eat it on my return."

23

A SECRET
REVEALED

Señor and Señora Marin omitted neither expense nor careful attention in their efforts to save the sick woman, but, unfortunately, she continued to grow worse, and the end was approaching.

Lucia and her husband were conversing together quietly: "How mysterious these things are, Fernando. Marcela came to our tranquil happy home seeking relief, which she found in the name of charity; we took pleasure in doing good, and, from those actions—good, elevated, and holy—resulted misfortune for all."

"Remember, my dear, that our work in life is to fight, and that the sepulchre of good is dug by ignorance. The triumph consists in not allowing ourselves to be interred."

Margarita appeared at the door like a meteor crying: "Señora, señora, my mother calls you!"

"I am coming," answered Lucia, leaving the room immediately. She found Marcela in a half sitting position, propped up by pillows.

On seeing Lucia, Marcela's eyes filled with tears, and in a broken, trembling voice, she exclaimed: "Señora Lucia, I am dying! Alas! my daughters . . . Doves without a nest . . . without a tree to shelter them . . . without a mother. Alas, alas."

"Poor Marcela, you are weak; do not agitate yourself; I will not preach to you, to try to prove or explain the mysteries of God, but you are good, you are a Christian," said Lucia, arranging the covers of the bed, slightly disordered.

"Yes, Señora."

"If your hour has come, Marcela, go calmly! Your daughters are not birds without a nest; this is their home, and I will be their mother."

"May God repay you . . . I wish to reveal . . . to you . . . a secret . . . to be lost in your heart . . . until the needful hour," gasped the sick woman, making a great effort to speak.

"What is it?" asked Lucia coming closer.

Marcela, putting her icy lips to the ear of Lucia, murmured

some phrases which caused the latter to start and look at the sick woman in wonder.

"Will you promise, señora?"

"Yes, I swear to you by Christ our Lord who died on the cross," responded Lucia, greatly moved.

And the poor martyr, whose last hour was approaching, added with a deep sigh which seemed to be her final farewell to the things of earth, "May God repay you! Now I wish to confess; death is awaiting me."

The arrival of Don Pascual was announced. Lucia, leading Margarita by the hand, returned his salute very coldly.

The priest approached the bed to listen to the sacramental confidences of his victim!

Margarita could not deceive herself any longer; her eyes were red with weeping. She would weep still more when she should see her mother carried out by strangers to be laid forever in the damp ground of the cemetery. Poor Margarita! Nevertheless, in her grief, she did not measure the magnitude of her misfortune. Lucia took the girls away and left them with a servant to put on the new dresses that had been made for them, saying to herself as she left: "The adorable simplicity of children. Ah! Childhood is gilded by the warmth of the refulgent sun of faith, while old age is frozen by the coldness of scepticism, knowing mankind as it is."

She found Don Fernando in his office. Almost at the same moment Manuel and Don Sebastian arrived. When Lucia saw them she said to herself wonderingly: "What is going to happen to-day in this house, where in these few days have taken place such tragic events, the extent of which it is impossible to measure? What new drama is going to unfold itself in my home where an invisible hand has brought together now the principal actors, persecutors and persecuted; guilty and innocent; in the presence of a mother who finds herself on the borders of a sepulchre opened for her by these notables—representatives of the church and of the authority?"

"I salute you, Señora Lucia," said Manuel, meeting her at the door of the study, which they entered, followed by Don Sebastian.

"Gentlemen," said Lucia, with manifest displeasure at the sight of Don Sebastian who, taking off his hat, said: "Good afternoon, madam."

"How do you do, Manuel; good afternoon, Don Sebastian!" said Don Fernando, repressing the strong feeling which the presence of the latter roused within him.

But Manuel, having anticipated that feeling, in order to relieve the difficult situation, was the first to commence the conversation, saying: "Señor Fernando, we have come to consult with you as to the manner in which you may receive the most explicit satisfaction from people who have offended you with the same ignorance with which a mad dog offends."

"To satisfy me is not a difficult thing, Don Manuel. I have studied more or less the character of this people, which is unfolding without the stimulus of good example, or of healthy advice; and which, at the cost of their own dignity, will still continue to preserve what they call their legendary customs.

"But how will they repair the damage inflicted on so many victims?" replied Señor Marin, giving to his words the severe accentuation of truth and reproach.

"And, really," Don Sebastian dared to inquire with trembling voice, "how many deaths have there been?"

"What! Do you not know, Don Sebastian, and you, a local authority? A very strange thing!" was all the reply that Don Fernando made as he went over to his wife.

"This seeming strangeness will be explained, Don Fernando, when it is known that my father has not gone out of his house since those terrible events which I had the good fortune to restrain, the lieutenant governor having taken charge of the post as the law provides."

"This precautionary and well-meditated action does not save him from responsibility," observed Lucia with her natural feminine vivacity.

Manuel replied readily: "Señora, I, having arrived at such a tragical time for Killac, for this my native town, could not remain indifferent. I must look for reparation; must seek to prevent new evils; therefore I have persuaded my father to resign the post he did not know how to sustain. I am going to try to repair some of the evil done."

"Are you going to enter into combat with vices which enjoy the privilege of being well rooted; with errors which increase and become fruitful under the protecting tree of custom, without some good example, some stimulus to awaken souls from the debility in which abuse has sunk them; the desire for immoderate gain and the ignorance preserved by speculation? It seems to me a difficult thing, Manuel," said Señor Marin.

Manuel was neither defeated nor convinced, and replied: "That is precisely the conflict of the Peruvian youth exiled in these retired regions; I have the hope, Señor Marin, that the civilisation which they seek, waving the banner of a pure Christianity, will not be long in manifesting itself, constituting the felicity of the family and, as a logical consequence, the felicity of society."

"And your strength will be sufficient, think you, Manuel? Can you count on other support than that which your noble mother offers, and we as friends can give?" asked Don Fernando.

Lucia crossed her arms as if tired and Don Sebastian remained firm as a post, planted under his historic cape.

"It is my belief that these people have not yet touched the deepest depths of abjection; the masses are docile. The very event which we lament has proved it to me," replied Manuel.

"I do not contradict you, Manuel; but . . . ."

"Error also has a remedy, really," ventured Don Sebastian.

"That is true, when that error has not crossed the threshold of eternity; Don Sebastian, we have several wounded, four dead, and the unfortunate Marcela ready to expire, leaving her daughters, to sum up, orphans, widows."

"In what manner will you rectify these errors?" interposed Lucia.

Don Sebastian covered his face with both hands, like a condemned child, Manuel turned pale, wiping the profuse perspiration that bathed his brow, and the despairing cry of Margarita reached them all.

"Mercy! Mother! Help!"

"Let us go!" exclaimed Lucia, rushing from the room.

All hurried to the bedside of the martyr wife, whose life went out in a sigh. One tear shone upon her face, the last tear with which she said farewell to this valley of tears.

Marcela had flown to the serene regions of imperishable peace leaving her mortal vesture behind, so that mankind might discuss in its presence the theory of organic decomposition that proclaims NOTHINGNESS and the principles of mechanical perfection driven by a SOMETHING, the activation and cessation of functions demonstrating the existence of a constructor's hand, thus revealing the Author of Nature!

There was the cadaver!

And Don Sebastian and the priest Pascual, the two men responsible for the sad event, stood in the presence of the spoils of death.

24
A SHOT
THAT
MISSED
ITS MARK

Tales and comments ran from mouth to mouth; some nearly exact, others greatly exaggerated. The Indians, ashamed of the docility with which they had responded to the alarm of the bells and had been deceitfully persuaded to attack the peaceful home of Don Fernando, wandered about the outskirts of the place moody and frightened.

Estéfano Benites gathered together his companions in the office of his house where we saw them before playing cards; seeing that his accomplices were vacillating, he said to encourage them: "Comrades, we must stand together!"

"I did not think the shot would go so far from the mark,"

said Escobedo, shaking a walking stick of *lloqque* that he was

holding.

"If the authorities come, you know what to do," instructed Estéfano.

"And if they make us declare, upon oath?" inquired Escobedo.

"We do not know anything. Comrades, remember, when the thing commences, it is not for nothing that I am secretary to the judge."

"Let us accuse the dead Indians," remarked one.

"We will put it upon the sexton; that Indian has cattle and can defend himself," was the advice of another.

"Man, did you speak to Champi that night?" asked Escobedo of the one who had spoken first.

"No, not I, it was Benites."

"Yes, I spoke with him," affirmed Estéfano.

"And how was it? I was thinking about calling Champi because he is a friend of mine and because I have pending a matter of grinding some wheat," said Escobedo interestedly.

"Well, what I said to him was this: 'Santiago, keep yourself ready, for from certain papers I know that a band of highwaymen has arrived on the outskirts of the town, robbing churches, and, as the service of the church is valuable, it must be guarded."

"Very good! Isidro thinks a great deal of me; is capable of following me to Purgatory, if need be," maintained Escobedo, smiling and tapping his *lloqque* against his feet.

"Do not forget to find out what is going on. I am going to Don Sebastian to take notes," said Benites, taking leave of his comrades, and each one went to his gossiping seat, as they called the corner of the plaza, a name which they themselves had given in a moment of inspiration.

The assault had taken place, just as had been arranged in the parochial house, but without the results aimed at by these blind followers of their vicious customs.

When the people were collected together, the house of Don Fernando was indicated to them as the refuge of the supposed highwaymen, and the moments of excitement of a mob are never those of reflection—they believed and attacked. That was how the tragedy came about.

Afterwards, the valiant words of a young man almost unknown to the people, followed by so respectable and beloved a lady as Doña Petronila, imposed the truce which was followed by a calm; and now, with that rapid change of popular sentiment, came the repentance—the horror—of what had already been done, which with the first rays of the morning light they contemplated as a most iniquitous farce.

The judicial authority appeared on the scene of disorder, and two wise men, appointed on the spot, gave in their report, in terms as technical as obscure, as to the investigation of the truth.

25
MARCELA
FOLLOWS
JUAN

On the entrance of Don Fernando, Lucia, Don Sebastian, and Manuel to the room of Marcela, who had just expired, the body, still warm, lay on a light iron bed.

Kneeling by the side of the bed, with his face hidden in his hands, was the priest Pascual.

Margarita, almost totally transformed, her hair loose, her eyes bathed in tears that sprang from her heart, clasped one of the hands of her dead mother. Lucia took a white handkerchief and covered the face of the one who had been Marcela, the Indian woman, with the respect which was inspired by that martyr of mother love, of gratitude and of faith.

Lucia's mind was filled with the revelation which Marcela had confided to her in her last moments.

Don Fernando and Don Sebastian remained in the middle of the room, and Manuel, gazing at Margarita, felt all the blood of his veins rushing to his heart.

Was it that he became acquainted with Margarita in such a solemn situation, and when his soul was predisposed by the rush of so many and varied sensations, that he became influ-

enced imperceptibly by the purest and grandest of passions?
Was it the confusion of sentiment and feelings, or the notable
beauty of Margarita that conquered the heart of the young student? We do not know, but Cupid had shot his dart through the
heart of Margarita and that of Manuel; and by the side of that
death-bed was born the love that was to conduct the young man
to the threshold of happiness.

In the death chamber, conversation is never very animated—
phrases uttered in an undertone, quiet steps, whisperings as if
still they were watching by a sick bed; such is the picture where
everything imitates the silence of the sepulchre.

This time it was Don Pascual who, rousing from his abstrac-
tion, with a wandering glance but clear voice, said: "Praise be to
God who, giving to-day glory to a saint in heaven, redeems a
sinner here on earth. My children! My children! Pardon! For I
promise in this august temple—here before the relics of a martyr—that for this sinner shall commence a new era."

Everyone remained stupefied and looked at Father Pascual,
wondering if he were crazy. But he, without taking notice, continued: "You cannot believe that in me should have died the
good seeds which the words of a Christian mother deposit in
the heart of a man. Unhappy is the man who is thrown into the
desert of the priesthood without the protection of a family! Pardon! Pardon!"

He fell again upon his knees, clasping his hands in attitude of
supplication.

"His mind is wandering," said one. "He has become insane,"
observed others.

Don Fernando, stepping forward, took the priest by the arm,
raised him up, and conducted him to his office to offer him a
place of rest.

Lucia, turning to those present and pointing to the lifeless
form, said: "Let us go, leaving in peace the remains of one who
is no more."

Manuel, taking Margarita by the arm, replied in a tender
tone: "Señora, if Marcela has gone away to heaven causing tears
to flow here, this child comes from there inspiring hope."

"Well said, Manuel. Margarita, if I could not make your mother's days pleasant, I will crown with happiness the years of your life; you shall be my daughter," said Lucia, turning to the orphan.

These words fell like refreshing rain upon the heart of the young man who, looking at Margarita, said to himself: "How beautiful! She is an angel? I also will work for her!"

"Come, let us go," repeated Lucia, taking the arm of Don Sebastian, who seemed to have become a statue of salt. "We have to fulfil the last duties for her who was Marcela," and she went out with Don Sebastian, leaving Manuel to follow with Margarita who, by a mysterious combination of circumstances, left the death chamber of her mother conducted by the man whom she was to love so much.

26
THE
PRIEST'S
CONFESSION

Positive is the sympathetic influence which can be exercised upon his fellow beings by a man who, recognising that he is working in a wrong path, turns and retraces his steps, asking the protection of the good.

For, heartless and selfish as may be the present century, it is false that the act of repentance does not inspire interest and merit respect.

The words of Father Pascual would have moved the noble sentiments of Don Fernando Marin to such a degree that he might be entirely disposed to support, or rather defend, the priest from the complications which might come upon him in the course of events, initiated by the intervention of the judge; but Señor Marin was a man of the world, acquainted with the human heart, and the attitude of Señor Pascual wore, for him, a different aspect than it would to ordinary people, and he said to himself: "This is the explosion of fright; the nervous shaking-up produced by fear; I cannot have faith in the words of this man."

Meanwhile the priest, as if divining by intuition the thoughts of Señor Marin, said to him: "I will not restrain myself, Don Fernando. Resolutions accompanied by vacillations come to nought. I have been more unfortunate than criminal. They are deceivers, those who, setting up an illusive theory, seek the virtue of the priesthood away from the family, thrown into the midst of their flocks when practise and experience, like the two hands of the dial which should indicate infallibly the hour, show us that it is impossible to obtain anything but the degeneration of man's nature."

"You might have been a model priest, Don Pascual."

"Yes, in the bosom of a family, Don Fernando, but to-day can I say it before you?—set apart in the priesthood, I am a bad father of children who cannot recognize me; the baneful recollection of women who never have loved me; a sad example for my parishioners! Alas! Alas!"

The voice of the man became choked; great drops of perspiration stood on his brow, and his glance inspired fear rather than respect.

"Calm yourself, Father Pascual! Why such excitement?" said Don Fernando with a gesture of compassion, while his countenance revealed his surprise, for the person before him was not the Father Pascual whom he had seen and talked with many times; it was the lion awakened from lethargy by the pain of a mortal wound, tearing himself in pieces.

"The revelation of Marcela!" exclaimed the priest, covering his face with his hands, then taking them away to raise them towards heaven as if overcome with terror.

Those words of sacramental revelation, were they of supreme importance? It would appear so.

Whatever they were, they fell upon a spirit already prepared by the terror which filled him at the result of the assault, and the undue excitement of the brain produced by the liquor and the pleasures he had drunk to the dregs in the arms of Melitona; added to these the words that Manuel hurled at him as a terrible reproach; all these must produce a terrible effect.

In such situations, a man goes to one or the other extreme of social life—virtue or crime.

But the entire organism of the priest was completely worn out and the reaction for good could not be expected to endure. That was the delirium-tremens that attacks the brain, showing him phantoms that speak and threaten. His lips were dry, his respiration fast; but he continued his discourses interrupted by an internal conflict.

"Woman is like honey . . . taken in large quantities, she destroys your health. . . . I am . . . resolved, Don Fernando!"

Father Pascual, now delirious, fell to the floor senseless.

They raised him up, already stricken with typhoid fever. It was necessary to send him to his home, lonely and desolate, without the affection and assistance of loving friends.

For the unhappy man there were no attendants except his *pongo* and *mitayas,* and no love except from his dog.

27
SEBASTIAN'S
BAD
CONSCIENCE

The high mountaintops that surround Killac were covered with that pale light which the king of day sometimes leaves behind him as he sinks in the west, and which the country people call the "sun of the gentiles."

The evening was tranquil; the tired husbandman was wending his way wearily homeward; the birds with drooping wing sought their sheltering tree, and the grasshoppers, flitting about, announced the coming of night with the monotonous zum, zum peculiar to them.

Lucia and Manuel, in the presence of Don Sebastian, were occupied in making the last arrangements for the interment of Marcela when Don Fernando entered.

"Fernando, what strange things are happening! Is poor Pascual still repentant?" asked Lucia.

"My dear, Father Pascual appears to be dying of fever, and in his delirium says things that make the soul shudder," replied her husband, passing his hand across his brow.

On hearing this, Don Sebastian jumped as if bitten by a viper, screaming: "May God protect and favour me! There is nothing now wanting but for the judges to come. Really, this is horrible! Horrible!" he repeated, beating his brow with the palms of his hands.

"Calm yourself, Don Sebastian. Do not make yourself ill!" said Don Fernando.

At that moment was heard the bell of the temple tolling for a death, and asking prayers for the soul of Marcela, wife of Juan Yupanqui.

Lucia, who was standing near Margarita, folded her to her heart saying: "Let us find your little sister Rosalia; it is some time since we saw her." Then, turning to her husband, she added: "Fernando; you finish here while I go to prepare a resting place for these two birds without a nest."

"Margarita, Margarita," murmured Manuel in the ear of the girl, "Lucia is your mother, I will be your brother." And a tear rolled down the cheek of the young man, like the precious pearl with which his heart repaid Lucia for the love and kindness shown to the poor orphan, whose altar of adoration was already raised in his soul with the white lilies of first love. To love is to live!

PART TWO

28
FERNANDO
AND THE
JUDGE

The heart of man is like a cloudy sky, alike in its tempests and in its serene calmness. How numerous are the phases through which it passes!

After the night of storm comes the clear sunlit day.

After the sad events which we have narrated in the first part of this history, the inhabitants of the little town of Killac entered into a period of calm similar to the languor that succeeds a period of immoderate work, although the tempest aroused in Manuel's heart was growing great, swelled by his solitude and idleness.

Months passed, and at last the case was called through, by which they pretended to wish to discover the guilty parties in the assault of the fifth of August.

The preliminary inquiries, with their legal technicalities, had not been sufficient to lay bare the truth, and they really have discovered nothing of what we already know—the case having been followed up with the slowness and carelessness characteristic of Perú, where crime is left unpunished and ofttimes innocence is threatened.

Notwithstanding, the pile of documents increased in dimensions daily, and further affirmations were added in which were noted the lengthy statements of witnesses who, even in giving their age, state, religion, etc., failed to speak the truth.

Señor Marin was summoned to the court to make a declaration and, notwithstanding his lack of interest in the case, he obeyed the summons and appeared before the Justice of the Peace, commissioned by the Recorder to prepare the *sumario*.

The Judge, Don Hilarion Verdejo, a man well advanced in years, thrice a widower, and the present proprietor of Manzanares, bought from the estate of the Bishop, Don Pedro Miranda y Claro, was gravely seated in his sanctum, before a pine table, in an easy chair of the kind manufactured some forty years ago, in Cochabamba, Bolivia, and now quite a rarity in the cities of Perú.

Two gentlemen accompanied Verdejo, who were to serve as witnesses to the "declaration." In the meantime Señor Fernando Marin, having arrived on the scene, was cordially welcomed by the Judge, who, extending his hand, said: "You will pardon me, Don Fernando, for having troubled you to appear; I would have called on you, but . . . in these times . . . there is really so much to do . . . I really . . ."

"Away with excuses, Judge, you are quite in order," replied Señor Marin; and Don Hilarion, without further parley, commenced the reading of documents which at once convinced Don Fernando of the absurdity on his part of continuing the case, in itself worthy of being treated by people of more thought and discretion as well as justice.

"Shall we get down to facts, Judge?" asked Don Fernando.

"Wait a little, my friend; my secretary will not delay long," replied Verdejo, somewhat disturbed, and adjusting his hat on a corner of the table, meanwhile directing furtive glances towards the door, through which at last appeared Estéfano Benites, carrying a quill over his right ear.

After a hasty greeting, drawing up his chair, he said: "I have been somewhat delayed, sir; kindly excuse me," and mechanically taking his pen, he placed himself in his accustomed attitude, ready to write at the dictation of Don Hilarion, who said: "Put down your heading, Don Estéfano, in a good hand, as it is a matter belonging to our friend Señor Marin."

Benites, after writing a few lines, replied: "It is down, sir."

Don Hilarion here coughed to clear his throat, and in solemn tones, or, rather, like a scholar repeating his lesson from memory, commenced as follows: "Interrogated as to whether he knows and is able to state that there have been disorders and riots with firearms, in this town, on the night of the fifth of August—"

"Yes, he knows, and is able to state the same, as his house was actually assaulted," Don Fernando hastened to reply, desirous of sparing the Judge difficulties in the editing of the report.

"With this declaration you completely annihilate your enemies, friend Marin," said Don Hilarion with a parenthesis in his dictation.

Don Fernando limited himself to silence whilst the Judge continued: "Interrogated as to whether he knows who attacked the house, or who were perpetrators of the assault . . ."

"Yes!" said Don Fernando with firmness.

At such a reply Estéfano raised his countenance, shewing thereon the undisguised astonishment, consequent on such an unexpected blow, and looked clearly at Señor Marin, although he failed to discover anything by which he might suspect that his participation in the affair was known to Señor Marin.

From that moment his handwriting changed in a marked degree, and showed plainly that he was under strong excitement. The witnesses exchanged significant glances which the Judge did not fail to observe.

"That being so, we shall catch the criminals," and thinking he had done sufficient work, the Judge added: "That will do for to-day, Don Fernando; to-morrow we will continue, all being well, for I have an appointment. Alas! What a busy life is that of a judge, and still no . . . ," he said, scratching the palm of his left hand with the fingers of his right.

"Just as you please, Judge; there is nothing urgent on my part," responded Señor Marin, taking up his hat and bowing himself out. As he was leaving, Estéfano accosted him with an air of mystery, saying in an undertone: "Señor Marin, excuse me; but who will pay my fee as Secretary?"

"I do not know, my young friend," answered Don Fernando, with a shake of the head, and forthwith retreating.

As soon as they were alone, Verdejo observed, addressing his Secretary: "So he said he knew them, eh?"

"Yes, Don Hilarion. But that is only his word," replied Benites, cleaning his pen with a bit of paper.

"And, now that I remember—so that all may be in perfect order—we must immediately decree the *embargo* on the stock of the sexton Champi, for up to the present he is the only one compromised in this affair," following out his preconceived plan.

"Aha! I was forgetting. Make out the decree, and strong too!"

Thus authorised, Benites at once drew up a species of order of sale on the cattle, sheep, and alpacas of Isidro Champi, sexton of Killac, to whom that stock represented untold sacrifices made by him and his family during all their life-time.

After writing, Estéfano consulted the Judge saying, "The Depository exacted by the law can be our friend Escobedo; he is a person of good standing, honourable, and altogether with us, Judge."

"Escobedo?" repeated Don Hilarion scratching his ear, and after a slight pause, said: "Yes, that will do—put down Escobedo."

Having arranged the scattered documents upon the table, Señor Verdejo took his hat to leave, his day's work being finished.

29
MANUEL,
A GOOD
TEACHER

The situation of Manuel was becoming very complicated. Shut up in his room for long hours, he often said to himself in his frequent soliloquies: "Although Don Sebastian's name has not yet appeared in the ordinance, it is in everyone's mouth, indicated for accusation and proof. The explanation which would be given of my conduct by outsiders who should see me frequent the house of Don Fernando could not be satisfactory at this time, and the comments that would be made, not honourable to me. I must be strong; I will make the sacrifice that I may one day be worthy of her. I will not visit the house; but what sad moments this keeping away imposes upon me, when my heart belongs to Margarita and my ardent desire is to participate in the plans that the Señora Lucia projects for the educa-

tion of the orphans. Sorrow of the soul! Thou art called Fate
and I am thy son!"

So saying, he buried his face in his hands, seeming like one
who sinks himself in a shoreless sea of doubt and meditation.
He remained thus for a long time, then arose quietly with the air
of one who had come to a decision.

Manuel evidently had a plan formed in his brain, dictated,
without doubt, by his heart, and soon began to prepare the
ground for the realisation of his ideas.

One day, after hesitating a long time, sentiment conquered
his will, and he said: "It is time to leave all comment on one
side. Tonight I go."

For the first time since his arrival in Killac, Manuel devoted a
great deal of time and care to his toilette. The gloves kept for
his examinations at the University were taken from the depths
of his trunk, and every portion of his dress arranged with
scrupulous care. Then he went to the garden to pass away the
time. Thoughts of Margarita mingled with the brightness and
perfume of the flowers. With his whole being absorbed in illusive dreams he gathered a bunch of violets and hid it carefully in
the inner pocket of his coat, saying to himself:

"The violets are flowers that represent modesty, and that is a
virtue which enhances the loveliness of a beautiful woman. Violets for my Margarita! When at my age they gather them in the
midst of the rays of light that illuminate the enamoured heart,
involuntarily they leave a piece of the soul in each flower, so that
all united together, it may fly to join the soul of the loved being.
The age of twenty—they say—is the poetry of existence; the
flowers are its rhymes; love its own life. Oh! I feel, I know that
since I have loved I live."

At last the long-desired hour arrived, and Manuel, pulling on
his gloves and applying cologne to his clothes, set out on his
way through the deserted streets of Killac, the uneven pave-
ments of which he covered with gigantic strides, arriving at the
house of Don Fernando with his heart palpitating with emotions that for him breathed of nectar and ambrosia.

On entering the reception room he found Lucia putting in
the last stitches to a watch pocket of blue satin on which she

had embroidered with shaded silks a forget-me-not with her husband's initials on the other side. Seated near her was Margarita, more beautiful than ever, her hair loose, confined only in front by a ribbon. She was engaged in putting away in a pasteboard box the pieces of a dissected alphabet, of which she already knew the different letters.

Rosalia, playing with another little girl of her own age, was laughing merrily at a rag doll, the face of which she had just washed with some tea which had been left in a cup.

Manuel remained a moment contemplating that beautiful family picture, where Margarita represented to his heart the angel of felicity.

Lucia turned her head, expecting to see Don Fernando, but, on seeing Manuel, said in surprise: "Oh! Is it you, Manuel?"

"Good evening, Señora Lucia! I have surprised you! Am I back from the dead?"

"Do not say that! If I was surprised it was because you have been lost for so many days," she replied, responding to his salutation and inviting him to be seated.

"All the more reason why you should have lived in my memory and heart," replied the youth, and as he spoke he looked towards Margarita, whom he greeted by saying: "And how is the happy godchild?"

And he took her little hand, and as it brushed against his it aroused in both young people the affection of two souls entering into contact.

"Very well, Manuel. I know all the letters now."

"Very good. Let me examine you," and taking up the box he began to show her the letters.

"A, Y, D, M," said the girl quickly.

"You pass!" said Lucia, laughing.

"Now you must combine them. I will be your teacher," proposed Manuel. Taking six letters, then nine, and arranging them in order, said: "Look!" and he made her spell.

"M-a-r-g-a-r-i-t-a! M-a-n-u-e-l!"

Lucia understood the intention of Manuel and said smilingly: "Good teacher! He does not forget his own interests; wishes to engrave his name in the memory of his pupils."

"My audacity goes still further, señora. I would like to en- grave it in the heart also," said Manuel laughing.

Margarita did not take her eyes from the letters. Without venturing a bet, we feel safe in saying that she already knew how to join those two names.

Manuel, quite impressed by the turn matters were taking, to conceal his emotion, asked carelessly: "Señora, is Don Fernando at home?"

"Yes, he is. When you entered I thought it was he. He will be in soon now. But, to return to the other subject, why have you kept away from us for so long?" asked Lucia.

"Señora, I do not wish to offend you by painful explanations. I have thought it prudent to do so while these judicial proceedings were going on."

"You are very thoughtful, Manuel; but we know all about it . . . that you saved us."

"Not for you, but for others," Manuel hastened to say, noticing the interest with which Margarita listened to the words of her godmother.

At this moment Don Fernando entered, saluting Manuel cordially.

30
COLONEL
PAREDES

Father Pascual was almost miraculously saved from the attack of typhoid fever which kept him prostrated some days, in the bed of pain, cared for by charity. His convalescence was slow, notwithstanding the mildness of the climate and the abundance of milk and other nutritious food.

The condition of his brain called for a change of scene, of objects and customs, in order to be dispossessed of all those terrible images which filled him with terror and remorse.

He resolved to go to the city to consult a doctor and seek comfort, leaving his parish temporarily in the charge of a Franciscan friar who arrived at Killac about the same time as the new authority named by the supreme government to rule the province entered into his duties.

Well chosen was the Colonel Bruno Paredes, a man well known in all parts of Perú. He enjoyed a great fame for his ability to sustain his part at banquets, as well as to keep his coffers well filled by the fruits of his office. Paredes was also an old comrade of Don Sebastian, companion-in-arms in some old revolution years before.

Don Bruno was nearly sixty years of age, well preserved; his personal appearance somewhat improved by a certain kind of hair dressing and by the good offices of a dentist in Lima; tall and stout, with coarse features and colour more than modest. When he laughed boisterously the dentist's work was plainly visible. His lips were well protected by a moustache groomed to bristle out bulkily. He wore black pants, a blue jacket buttoned up to the collar with yellow dress-uniform buttons, of which he displayed more, only larger, on his dark brown frock coat, with enormous cord button loops, designating the rank of colonel; he also wore a broad-brimmed black wool hat, with a miniature metal horse adorning the wide hatband of striped grosgrain. He wore the uniform of a colonel although he had never troubled himself with any kind of military studies, but circumstances gave him the opportunity to put on the straps, and his candour was not sufficiently strong to enable him to despise them. His education and manner of speaking were of the worst kind.

On arriving at Killac he immediately sought out his old comrade, Don Sebastian. Knowing all that had occurred in the place, he began with all his customary frankness. "How is it, Don Sebastian, that you, a man of weight and authority, have allowed yourself to be led by a school-boy like Manuel; that is the last thing that should happen."

"Colonel, really, I declare to you that I could not do any other way. That boy has talked me completely over, and Petronila has clinched the nail with her tears."

"What a pretty state of affairs! You permit yourself to be led by the tears of a woman, and we will see how the country will go on. No, señor. You stand upon your own feet and I will support you, yes, señor."

"But my resignation is already in the office of the Prefect, really, Colonel."

"You talk like a child, Don Sebastian. Do you not know that it is the child with a godfather who is baptised? Where is your courage of former times?"

"But how shall we arrange matters? Really, this is serious," said Don Sebastian joyfully.

"We will arrange it in two minutes; yes, señor; you can withdraw your resignation or not, and I will name you Governor again; yes, señor," said the Colonel, putting both hands in his pockets and marching up and down the room.

"Really, Colonel," observed Don Sebastian, passing his hand through his hair as if seeking ideas. "Easter is near, and we can send a yearling to the Prefect; but, really, Colonel, what about Manuel?"

"Oh, laugh at Manuel! You need not tell him anything about it. And, making use of our former frankness, I am going to tell you clearly that I need you, Don Sebastian. I need your support, I have come counting on you. This Sub-Prefecture must get me out of certain tight places, yes, señor. You know a man has to spend something, and for five years I have been trying to obtain this place, as you know, and my plans are well thought out."

"Ah, that gives another aspect to the matter," replied Don Sebastian.

"And did you think me an idiot? When one hires a milch cow, she is returned quite dry. My efforts have not been slight to obtain this post."

"That is very true, Colonel. But what about the judgment in that matter of the attack?"

"About the judgment? Ha! ha! ha! How plainly it is to be seen that you are a novice in these things. Afraid of the judgment! Let your great-great-grandchildren say that it is null and void, and let us not think anymore about it. And how is our priest Pascual?"

"Our priest has gone to the city. Really, he nearly died."

"I am sorry, because the priest would have been of great assistance in the carrying out of our projects. We have to gather up a good number of dollars this year," said Don Bruno, taking his hands out of his pockets.

"Of course, Colonel; really, Father Pascual suited us, so good, so condescending as he was."

"And continues to be as loving as ever?"

"That, Colonel, is a habit he will have down to the grave, and, really, one is a man. . . ."

"Yes, señor, one is a man. And Estéfano Benites and other friends here?" inquired Don Bruno with interest.

"All well, Colonel, and, really, Benites pleases me very much."

"Well, summon them, Don Sebastian. I wish to leave all our plans of administration definitely arranged, so that I may go on my way, for I must not delay taking the oath of office."

"This instant, Colonel; although, really, they will not delay in coming to congratulate you; they already know of your arrival in town," replied Don Sebastian, feeling entirely reanimated.

All the scruples which the words of Manuel had raised in his soul had disappeared under the influence of the words of Colonel Paredes, with the same rapidity with which the clouds of sunset fade, or good ideas when faced with the superior moral position of those who fight against them.

31
TIRED OF
KILLAC

Manuel's visit to Don Fernando's house resolved one of the important issues in his life, as will be seen.

Don Fernando related to Manuel what had occurred at the Courthouse, adding: "And does not all this give you a sad idea of what these authorities are, Manuel?"

"Don Fernando, my soul is wounded to the quick, and every new detail is like putting a finger into the sore. Ah! If I could only take my mother away!" said the young man earnestly.

"For this, Manuel, we have resolved to send the children somewhere else to be educated," said Lucia.

"And what place have you selected?" he asked quickly.

"Lima, of course," replied Don Fernando.

"Oh, yes, Lima! There they educate the heart and instruct the intelligence. And then, I believe that in a few years Margarita will find a good husband. With that face and those eyes she will not remain long single," said Lucia, laughing happily.

But Manuel, turning pale, inquired, "Have you decided yet on the date of departure?"

"We have not settled the exact date, but it will be this year," replied Don Fernando.

"Going to Lima is like reaching the antechamber of Heaven, and viewing the throne of Glory and Fortune. They say that our beautiful capital is like the city of the gods," said Manuel, trying to hide his emotion and resolving in his own mind to follow Margarita to Lima as soon as possible.

Lucia went over to speak apart with her husband, and Manuel took this time to give his bouquet of violets to Margarita, saying in a low tone: "Margarita, these flowers are like you; I hope to find you always as modest as they. Keep them."

Margarita nimbly took the little bouquet and hid it in her bosom with the agility with which a child hides a toy coveted by another.

Why does love start out with this instinctive stealth? Why does the flower of mutual attraction bloom amid the weeds of selfishness, dissembling, and falsity? Who could have told Margarita that it was a forbidden act to accept the flowers a young man offered her, glistening with the dew of affection?

It is the mystery of souls!

This statement could be read in the fire in the eyes of Manuel, who, with his phosphorescent eyes, was to set ablaze the girl's heart—a virgin heart beginning to feel those slight quiverings that, not even noticed at first, eventually leave in the eyelashes a tremulous tear, wrenched out of her by love. Tears of happiness! Tears which announce to the heart the hour of sentiment; the rain that bedews the flower of hope. The heart of woman is the heart of a child from birth to death, unless frozen by the terrible tempests of unbelief or depravity.

Lucia, changing the theme of conversation, said to her husband: "Do you know, Fernando, that Manuel has a thousand scruples about continuing to visit us?"

"For us, my dear, there is no reason why he should have any scruples, but for others, he is right; nevertheless," he added, turning to Manuel, "you could come in the evening."

"Many thanks, Señor Marin."

"And they tell me that the new authority has arrived. Do you know, Manuel, where he is staying?"

"Yes, señor, he was at our house to-day, but continued his journey immediately. I saw and saluted him in passing, but I think we do not sympathise with each other. He knew me as a child."

"I am sorry. A youth like yourself is worth more than twenty old men of that type. I do not wish to flatter you, but think the authority would gain by your friendship."

"Thanks for so much kindness, Don Fernando; but those who know us when children seldom wish to see us at any other time," replied Manuel, taking his hat to leave.

When the "Good-nights" were said, Margarita added: "You will come again, Manuel, will you not?"

The young man was soon traversing the gloomy streets of Killac, the silence of which would inspire fear in the hearts of anyone who remembered the tragic scenes of the fifth of August and the picture of the death of Juan Yupanqui.

But Manuel was too much occupied with other thoughts to think of those things now. He walked on, thinking aloud: "Yes, I will go to Lima! Within three years I shall be a lawyer, and Margarita a beautiful woman, good and noble. And then, will she return my love? or will she look upon me as the son of the man who caused the death of her parents? Thank God, for the first time in my life I feel satisfied with my true father. But why cannot I bear his name—the name that all respect and love? It is not the command of God; it is human aberration and weakness, a cruel law! Margarita mine! I will declare all to Don Fernando and then you shall be my wife. Love will stimulate my aspirations. I will be a lawyer as soon as possible. I shall go to the famous San Marcos University and study day and night. A person with will and determination can accomplish anything. She must love me; she accepted my violets and asked me to come again. If she were a woman, I could reveal my thoughts to her. But

Margarita is still a child, and that child has robbed me of my heart. Yes, I will be worthy of the godchild of the good Señora Lucia!"

So thinking, Manuel arrived at his home, where his mother awaited him.

Manuel appeared to be completely insane; he was speaking aloud with such fire just as the barking of a dog that was threatening to devour the calves of his legs brought him out of his state, and made him notice that he was at the door of his house, which was open for him, since the affection of Doña Petronila was awaiting his return with the supreme love, that of a mother, willing to keep watch at night and make sacrifices.

Things were not at ease in that house, since as soon as Manuel set foot in the vestibule, he found his home astir with an agitated hubbub.

32
NO NEED
OF A
WARRANT

As Don Sebastian expected, the neighbours, or a certain class of them, gathered together quickly as soon as the news of the arrival of the Sub-Prefect was spread over the town. The Sub-Prefect, Don Bruno Paredes, was seated in Don Sebastian's reception room, ready to receive them. The greetings were profuse and hearty.

"We are very glad to see you among us!" "Now we shall have good administration!" "All the prominent neighbours of the place congratulate you."

So ran the chorus of voices, to which the Colonel replied: "I come with the best intentions, with the firm purpose of supporting the people of the locality."

"That is what we wish!" exclaimed several voices at once.

Just then Estéfano Benites appeared.

The Sub-Prefect added: "As for me, I hope you will back me also, gentlemen. . . . Why, hello to my friend Benites," Don Bruno said, spotting the new arrival.

"Count on us, your honour, 'Usía (Your Honour),'" answered Benites, brimming with joy.

"Yes, 'Usía,' we are with you," said several voices.

"I am going to leave my instructions with the Governor and expect that my friends will support and stand by him," indicating Don Sebastian.

"Will Don Sebastian continue to be Governor?"

"Yes, gentlemen. I think you will be satisfied with him."

"Yes, that is what I said would suit us," said Estéfano Benites, looking from one to another.

"Well, we must take advantage of the times to make our assessment moderate, eh! In legal business I do not like abuses," said the Colonel warily, looking at the wall.

"Yes, that is just, and that is the custom of all the sub-prefects," said Don Sebastian.

"It is a good custom and protected by the Indians buying here," added Escobedo.

"And have you heard about the trouble with Don Fernando?" inquired Estéfano, in order to know what course to pursue.

"I know a great deal about it, but you people have been badly advised; things are not done in that way. Another time you must act more . . . prudently," said the Sub-Prefect, revising his answer in mid-sentence, since he realised he had been about to say something he would regret.

"That is what I explained to them, but the sexton is the one to blame, ringing the bell and rousing the people," said Estéfano, winning the admiration of his colleagues, who said:

"That is the truth, it says so in the report."

"And has that already been proved in the investigation?"

"Yes, señor, and up to now no measures have been taken against that Indian sexton, and only the names of respectable persons are mentioned," replied Estéfano.

And Don Sebastian added: "Really, Colonel, if it had not been for the action of the sexton, nothing would have happened, because, really, Don Fernando is a good man."

"And who is the sexton?" inquired Don Bruno.

"An Indian, Isidro Champi, your excellency, a very plain, simple man, who would like to think he is somebody, because he has many animals," said Escobedo.

"Then, my Governor, do you order the arrest of Isidro Champi at once; put him in prison at the disposition of the Justice, and on my return we will arrange matters," said the Sub-Prefect.

"That is it. We must proceed with energy and justice," observed Estéfano.

"Magnificent! Really, the Indian Champi should pay for his fault," added Don Sebastian.

"Very well. Now I must leave. My horse?" said the Colonel going to the door.

During this meeting, the agents and commissaries of Don Sebastian had prepared a grand guard of honour to accompany the Sub-Prefect on his departure; and in the yard were found many horses saddled and a band of music awaiting the coming forth of the hero. An *alcalde* in ceremonial garb, with his vicuña threads worked into his braid, was holding the reins of the spirited sorrel horse of Colonel Don Bruno Paredes.

In the street was a crowd of masked Indians wearing skirts, with a coloured handkerchief crossed at the shoulder, carrying another handkerchief fastened to a long pole which they waved to the sound of the drum as they danced for the Sub-Prefect, and followed the march of the escort.

"Long live the Sub-Prefect, Colonel Paredes!!"

"Viva—a—a—a!!!" shouted a chorus of hoarse voices.

The Sub-Prefect heard, with great satisfaction, his name applauded by that miserable crowd, puffed up, like the frog in the fable, filled with vanity as is every one who reaches by foul means an unmerited position, and with a brilliant cavalcade the brave Colonel pursued his journey.

Don Sebastian made signs to Estéfano to remain after the others had left, and they plotted together how best to carry out the orders of the Sub-Prefect.

"Well, Don Estéfano, really; you have excelled yourself this time," said Don Sebastian.

"I am glad that my remark proved to be such a good shot," replied the young man with satisfaction.

"Yes, indeed; we shall save ourselves; with the Indian Champí fast in jail there will be no one to say anything."

"That is so. Now let us indite the warrant."

"No need of a warrant, Estéfano. Go you with two officers and arrest him, and take him to jail; everyone heard the order of the Sub-Prefect," said the Governor, and Estéfano, well content, went out to do his work.

Don Sebastian remained alone; but he was not happy. He knew that a new domestic battle must ensue; his wife and son would surely begin to reason with him and perhaps defeat the new phantasm of ambition, in whose arms dreamt sweet illusions, swelling the heart of the ex-Governor with the heartening promises of Colonel Paredes and the quick thinking of Estéfano Benites.

Would he fall again defeated, sadly defeated?

It was necessary to take arms and be at the ready. For this, Don Sebastian appealed to the supreme reinforcement of cowards, and, striking the table with his fist, he said imperiously:

"What is all this now? Really, I am no child anymore! *Pongo!*" he shouted with all the grace of a man with a few coins on his person, and his order was answered by the Indian, who appeared in the door and was ordered by Don Sebastian:

"Step lively now, tell Doña Rufa to send me . . . really, a bottle, the best."

The Indian went out like a flash, returning instantly with the bottle and a glass.

The Governor served himself a respectable ration and drank it quickly, saying: "Now let them come; we will meet them face to face."

That which Don Sebastian drank was not the juice of the grape, but alcohol of the sugar cane slightly diluted with water. Its effects are almost instantaneous, dominating the reason and the brain, taking away the man and leaving the brute.

Doña Petronila observed attentively all that occurred at the house since the coming of the new authority, before whom, however, she did not present herself. When she saw the *pongo* enter

her husband's room with the provision of drink, her first impulse was to take it away from him and destroy it. But her good
sense came to her aid and taught her to refrain. "It will be better
to wait until Manuel comes. He will know better what to do,"
she said.

The night was advancing.

Suddenly a hoarse voice was heard. "What do you want?
Really, no one is going to order me around!"

And just then a noise was heard like a chair being knocked
over violently.

Doña Petronila came running into the room and stood contemplating for some seconds Don Sebastian, who continued to
yell like a madman:

"Yes, sir! Really, no one . . . I take orders from no one!"

His tongue balked at enunciating the words clearly and he
was unsteady on his feet. When Don Sebastian made out Doña
Petronila, he immediately shouted:

"Here's the beast . . . ! Fire, sir, really . . . !"

And, seeing a chair, he threw it towards his wife.

Doña Petronila, her expression unchanged, replied:

"My good man, it seems you do not know me. . . . I'll take
you to bed . . . it is late."

And grasping him by the arm she tried to lead him; but Don
Sebastian, taking this as an act of despotism, shook her off, and
grabbing hold of the now-empty bottle, and everything else he
could lay hands on, he threw it all at Doña Petronila, shouting
and making an infernal noise:

"Devil of a woman . . . ! No . . . , really, no one puts the bit in
my mouth!"

"Good God, what has been going on?"

"I'm Governor and that's that, like it or not!"

"What is all this? What has gotten into this town? Sebastian,
for God's sake, calm down," said Doña Petronila again in tones
of supplication.

But Pancorbo, with a drunken stubbornness, replied:

"I take orders from no one, hear?"

And another chair crashed near Doña Petronila, who was dodging back and forth, wiping her tears with a corner of her shawl.

The disturbance brought several neighbours running, and just then Manuel also realized something was going on, ran in, seized hold of Don Sebastian around the waist, lifted him up to his own height, and carried him off to his bedroom.

33
THE
WRONG
ONE
IMPRISONED

Estéfano quickly found his men and went with them to the poor hut of Isidro Champi, who was just taking leave of his family to go to the tower to be ready to ring the "Hail Mary," which is tolled on the large bell at twilight.

Isidro Champi, nicknamed Tapara, was a tall strong man of some forty years of age, with a wife and seven children, five boys and two girls. He wore black pantaloons with red stripes, waistcoat and shirt of scarlet, and a light green jacket. His long thick hair, braided and tied with ribbons woven of vicuña threads, hung in a low plait down his back; his head was covered with a graceful Spanish cap, much used by the Indians because they love to dress up in costume and wear bright colours.

The appearance of Estéfano and his men in the house of Isidro greatly alarmed the Indian family because they were accustomed to looking upon a visit from that class of persons as a presage of some misfortune to be expected immediately.

Estéfano was the first to speak.

"Well, Isidro, you have to go to jail by order of the Sub-
Prefect."

If the house had been struck by lightning it would not have
produced the effect Benites' words did upon the Indians, watch-
ful and suspicious from the moment they saw the officers.

The women knelt before Estéfano, their hands clasped in
supplication, sobbing and moaning; the boys rushed to their father, and in the midst of the confusion Isidro could only mur-
mur: "*Ninoy wiracocha!* (Señor! Why?)"

"There is no need for all this noise; come along, and do not
be afraid," interrupted Estéfano. "It is nothing; we are going to
clear up the matter of the bell ringing."

On hearing this the clean conscience of Isidro gave him
courage, and turning to his wife he said: "Calm yourself, then,
and later on bring me my *poncho*,"* and went away resolutely
with the officers.

The heart of Isidro's wife could not be calm, because it was
the heart of a woman, a mother and a loving wife, who fears
everything when her own family are concerned.

Calling her eldest son she said to him: "Michael, did I not
tell you when the pot slipped and the milk soured that some
misfortune was going to happen to us?"

"Mamma, I have seen the raven pass five times over the roof
of the crib," said one of the five children.

"Is that true?" said the Indian woman, pale with terror.

"It is true, true, Mamma. What shall we do?"

"We will go to our friend Escobedo. He can speak for us,"
answered the mother, and, wrapping herself in a *lliclla* woven of
puito, she set out, followed by two shaggy dogs, whom Miguel
tried to call back home, whistling in a special way after he called
them by name:

"Zambito! Deserter! Wheehoo!" Zambito wagged his tail
and came home, but Deserter, more disobedient, or perhaps
more loyal to his mistress, followed after her, dangling his
tongue out from time to time and panting.

---

* A long shawl with a slit in the middle to pass the head through.

34

GOING
TO LIMA

Don Fernando began to be more and more troubled about the future that awaited him in Killac. He knew perfectly well that the apparent calm that reigned was not to be trusted. He was in the practise of paying for secret investigations, and he was aware of what was going on in the area, although he did not pass it along to Lucia because of her delicate condition.

Providence was going to bless their home with a new treasure, and this circumstance made the future father think frequently of the need to make a definitive decision. He continued to hesitate for three months after the time when Manuel came to visit and left with his mind spinning with projects.

"Margarita's progress, Rosalia so docile and promising to be a good girl, Lucia's condition; I see my family evolving into a charming new phase. I must not throw away this opportunity; I must be as happy and successful as I can be in life with a wife like Lucia. I need to make up my mind!"

At that very moment, the new authority, duly sworn by law, was touring the towns within his jurisdiction, where his subordinates offered him succulent dinners, supported by the Indians who were required to contribute the provisions.

The nation of Perú was being stirred by issues of great importance: nothing less than the election of the President and members of the national legislature.

When Don Fernando found out that the Killac sexton was lying buried in jail, he trembled, more in indignation than in horror.

"Here is the weak, the defenceless man, and he is the one who will feel the blade sharpened for the guilty," he said, just as the voice of fate echoes through the fatherland, telling of the bloody sacrifice of the Gutiérrez brothers; this injustice covered the face of civilisation with a cloud of human ashes.

So hearing about the sexton made Don Fernando tremble. He harboured well-founded suspicions that there could be another assault like the one the night of the fifth, because he was

not unaware of the promising words that Colonel Paredes had
spoken during his exchange with Don Sebastian. Later the deep
melancholy evinced by Manuel, who maintained a studied reserve, confirmed his judgment, since he guessed that a tenacious
struggle was underway between the young law student and Don
Sebastian. At the same time, suspicion sprang up in Señor
Marin's mind: this honest, gentlemanly young man could not be
the son of the unscrupulous, corrupt Governor of Killac.

When Don Fernando entered his wife's bedroom, she was in
front of a full-length mirror whose limpid surface shone from a
perfectly varnished wardrobe of black mahogany. It offered the
portrait of the svelte figure of Señor Marin's wife, wearing a
generously cut robe and her blonde hair loose, flowing over her
shoulders in graceful silken waves.

She had just come from her bath.

As he crossed the threshold, Don Fernando was also dupli-
cated by the mirror. Catching sight of him, Lucia smiled and
turned to face the original, who was approaching to greet her
with an embrace.

"I come to give you some good news, my dear," he said
cheerily.

"Good news in these calamitous times? Where do you get it
from, Fernando?"

"From my own brain and will," replied he.

"That is clear, but please explain yourself."

"This place troubles our happiness. Lucia, you are going to
become a mother, and I do not wish that the first link in the
chain of our future happiness should find its life here."

"And what then?"

"We will leave here definitely within twenty days without
fail."

"As soon as that, Fernando?"

"I have it all thought out and have come to warn you to have
ready the few articles we need to take with us."

"But where are we going?"

"I am going to take you to the land of flowers, in the beautiful Peruvian capital, where you will dwell in happiness arranging the cradle of our child."

"To Lima!" cried Lucia enthusiastically.

"Yes, to Lima; and, afterwards, when the child we expect is strong enough to endure the long journey, we will take a trip to Europe."

"And Margarita and Rosalia? What will become of them without us? We must care for them from gratitude, Fernando."

"They are our adopted daughters; they will go with us to Lima and there, as we have already planned, we will place them in the college best adapted to form wives and mothers, without wasting their time in exaggerated repetition of words called prayers without idea or sentiment," replied her husband.

"Thank you, Fernando; how good you are."

At that moment two soft knocks were heard on the screen, and the graceful figure of Margarita, more beautiful than ever from the love and care she received, appeared at the door.

"Señor," said the girl, "Manuel is in the parlour and says he would like to speak with you, Don Fernando."

"Has he been waiting long?"

"Yes, señor."

Don Fernando went out, leaving Lucia and Margarita together.

Lucia gazed upon Margarita enraptured for some moments, saying to herself inwardly:

"Someone once said that women respond more than any other being to compliments and genteel treatment. Ah! My Margarita is the perfect illustration of this idea."

And she was right.

When woman is shown appreciation and feels valued, she experiences a one hundred per cent gain in beauty and moral qualities. If not, let us just think of those unhappy women, hounded in the intimacy of their homes by unfounded jealousy; worn out by their husbands' gluttony; reduced to breathing stale air and eating whatever is left; and we have before us the portrait of the unhappy woman, ill-humoured, pale, with circles under her eyes, through whose mind pass none but melancholy thoughts, and whose will to action sleeps in the lethargic dream of a swoon.

35
FATHER PASCUAL'S SOLITUDE

To maintain the continuity of our story's events, we must go back in search of the characters we left behind.

The lofty sentiments of Christian reform, the confession he made beside Marcela's death-bed, and the grave condition in which they took Father Pascual to his deserted house, naturally worked their effect on Lucia's generous heart, arousing in it a lively concern for the fate of that forsaken soul.

Killac's healer, skilled at combatting typhus, which was endemic to the region, treated and saved the patient, who, once he was pronounced convalescent, made plans to travel to the city, leaving an interim priest in his stead.

Once an individual's nature has been eaten away at by vice, it is almost impossible to fulfil for long the demands of moral sanctity.

He who has besmirched his youth in the mire of disorderly living, so remote from the joy to be found in the temperate pleasures of chaste love; he who has wasted his nervous energy in those material excitements that weaken the springs of the organism, leaving it without the strength or coordination to perform the functions for which Nature unerringly designed it, making it subject to that moral law that rules man's nature; he who makes ill use of brutal instinct and consumes his existence in libertine dissipation, is a gravely ill creature, who cannot regain the health he craves even when he resolves to do so.

Nevertheless, the rehabilitation of a man who has become an exile from the labours of the righteous is still possible when his heart has not yet experienced the paralysis of those delicate fibers that, with a sweet stirring, respond to the names of God, fatherland, family.

For several days, Father Pascual kept away from liquor and the friendship of women; and this sudden abstention greatly overexcited his nervous system, stimulating his capacity for fantasy, which during his journey through hills and grassfields offered him with increased vividness scenes that streamed before his eyes as rapidly as if conjured by art of magic.

Voluptuous apparitions, some with laughable physiognomies, others terrifying, indelibly marked as participants in an orgy; white-winged angels brandishing the green palm leaf of triumph and waving it over the immaculate countenance of a mother or a wife, beside her the child of holy matrimony or at the foot of an altar that bore inscribed upon it the name of God . . . ! Oh! . . . how many images passed through that brain about to tear itself apart in a battle of phantasmagoria.

If Father Pascual had been under the effects of an enervating, weak climate, he would have gone straight to the madhouse; but the frozen air of the Andes, giving tone to the organs of his brain, protected them against the violent tempests of an outright attack of madness.

Would this man emerge from the battle purified or a martyr?

That was Father Pascual, terrified at all he had witnessed and been a part of; unable to drive out of his ears the sound of Marcela's mysterious revelation; taking the true measure of his own conduct. He grew desperate and from the first wanted to flee the scene of his wretched deeds and, indeed, at the time we have examined his mental state, he would have liked to flee from himself.

Conscience, located in the respiration valve called the human heart, is that great argument to dissuade those unhappy beings who would decipher the problem of life with the nothingness of death. Conscience sometimes sleeps quietly, but when it awakens, it hammers unceasingly at the soul of man. Father Pascual could flee the scene of the crime, could roam the universe; but his inexorable judge spoke to him over and over again in the fearful language of remorse, for which there is no other reply but reform.

In this desolate frame of mind the priest was putting ever more distance behind him, to the even gait of his he-mule, until, coming to El Tigre, he caught sight of a roadside inn with its beautiful proprietress standing in the doorway.

He dug his spurs into the beast, and in ten minutes he was alighting and ordering a bottle of "refreshment," which he downed thirstily, not neglecting to offer one to the lady.

Farewell to all dreams of reform! The careless words of other days came to his lips and offended the ears of the proprietress; alcohol took up its old residence, and his reflective dreams were replaced by drunken delirium.

The innkeeper's husband, who was the local dispatcher for post horses, arrived and said:

"This gentleman is drunken out of his mind, so let us put him back in the saddle."

"Yes, Leoncito, when this happens the animal is wiser than the man, and will take him back where he belongs," said the mistress of the inn.

And so it was done.

When Father Pascual found himself back in the saddle, he sat up, and spurred and lashed his mount, which continued along the familiar route without protest.

That was the last stopping-place, and two hours later the traveller was arriving in the long-desired city, whose soaring towers and minarets were, to his eyes, yet more apparitions rising up like a threat. His reason was wavering between reality and illusion, when suddenly his mount gave a start and threw itself into a frenzy of leaping, bucking, and kicking.

The first thing to fly into the air was Father Pascual's hat. The animal became startled all over again at the sight of some fluttering banners; the rider bobbled and wove in his saddle for several minutes and then hit the ground senseless.

This happened near a convent of Franciscan friars. A number of curious onlookers gathered, and compassion prompted them to convey the stranger to the convent doors, where the charity of the friars took in the injured man.

The Superintendent was a grave, kind-hearted man. Only God knows what mysteries of goodness were hidden within his heart.

The friar had met Father Pascual several times while travelling through Killac; he gave him all needed assistance, and when the priest had recovered his senses said to him:

"God's mercy is great, brother," and he shewed him to a cell to rest.

In the silence of the cloister, Father Pascual once again found himself spiritually denuded; forsaken, absolutely alone in the world. But . . . no! His apparitions had followed him, and his feverish delirium returned with double force. Amid sobs and tears he muttered broken remorseful words.

"Yes, my God . . . ! you have made man sociable; You have placed in his heart the bonds of love, fraternity, and family. He who turns away from all that, who flees from Your work, execrates Your natural laws and . . . falls abandoned . . . as I did, isolated in a remote parish . . . .

"Who? Who has managed to hold steadfast after fleeing normal human company? . . . here! . . . in this solitude, in these stony cloisters! . . . how many . . . one? a thousand . . . ? Have they borne upon their brows the virginal diadem, whether healthy or diseased . . . ? No! No!" And he thrashed his hands in the air.

By now Father Pascual's words were incoherent.

His eyes were bloodshot, his lips dry, his breath was burning like the steam from a live coal dropped into water. The veins on his temples stood out starkly, and the thirst that consumed his breath made him reach for a glass of water he espied on the night table.

"This drink will keep life going," he said, seizing the glass with tremulous hands.

And, raising it to his lips, he was barely able to drink it for the convulsive chattering of his teeth on the rim of the glass. He drained it to the last drop, and struggling to put the glass back in place, he fell to the floor with a loud cry. Stretched out full length on the floor, his body was wracked with death throes, and as it let out a tenuous, final groan, his face remained fixed in the rigidity of death.

Someone passing nearby, hearing the cry, came in, and, finding the sick man stretched out upon the floor, rang the bell so violently that several monks, among them the Superintendent, came hurrying in.

"He has done himself some dreadful harm!"

"He is cold as ice, holy Father, let us absolve him," said another, quoting from the words of the sacrament.

"Gather the community; perhaps we can aid him in his final
hour," ordered the Superintendent while the others lifted the
body up onto the bed.

"Has he died already? Merciful God!" exclaimed the Superintendent, clasping his hands and raising his eyes to heaven.

"*Requiescat in pace!*" someone said, as if pronouncing absolu-
tion. Meanwhile, the community had gathered, and intoned the
song for the occasion, sprinkling the body with holy water.

The Superintendent, summoning a lay brother, said:

"Brother Pedro, prepare a shroud and go with Brother Cirilio
to make ready the burying-ground."

As he left the death-bed accompanied by another friar, the
two conducted this exchange:

"For all that the materialists proclaim the contrary in 'Force
and Matter,' the truth, reverend Father, is that the kind of death
a person dies, and the respects paid to his remains, compose an
epilogue to the life and character of the individual."

"According to this," said the other friar, pulling his hood
over his head, "Father Pascual must have been a good Christian,
since he died peacefully and found pious hands to bury him; yet
the things one hears about him, Father . . . ."

"God save us from sudden death; but, judging with Christian
charity, sincere repentance is the gateway to salvation, and that
priest may well have expired on the wings of contrition," replied
the Superintendent, covering his hands with the voluminous
sleeves of his long habit.

"Sudden death may be comfortable for an individual who
does not believe in the afterlife, or for a just man who is prepared to depart this life at any moment; but for those of us who
are neither prepared nor doubt that there exists in man an im-
mortal animating spirit, it is a terrifying truth that one dies as
one has lived," reflected the friar as they arrived at the Superintendent's cell, at whose door they went separate ways.

Those philosophers were unaware of the cruel moments that
Father Pascual underwent before giving up his soul to God. The
torture of his soul, as he grasped that he had once had before

him the opportunity to be a moral and useful man, had it not been for the aberrations of human laws, contrary to those of nature; his anguish, without a friendly hand to sweeten so much bitterness, nor a word to lighten his sufferings; could these have been the true pains he suffered during his protracted death throes?

The sudden death of Farther Pascual has been a genuine loss to us, since we had been hoping to derive more material from the further course of his life. Such is, however, the reality of human existence. Death attacks without warning and wounds at the very moment when existence is most needed, just when the strands of life are threaded into the warp and woof of society, and the social fabric is beginning to be woven into its diverse forms.

The only word we can utter over the solitary grave of that unhappy priest, without a legal family and without the bonds of affection that the law of men tore away from him, is the laconic:

Rest in peace!

Let us return to Killac.

36
TALKING
IT OVER

Given Don Sebastian's weakness of character, after the meeting he had with the Sub-Prefect and the incident with Doña Petronila, it was only natural that his situation should grow more complicated.

Very humiliating for Manuel were the scenes that took place in Don Sebastian's bedroom, when Manuel carried him there by force to protect his mother from a drunken man.

Nonetheless, Manuel realized that there are family scenes that, if they happen under the paternal roof, are no lasting shame; and so he endured with manly stoicism a stream of invective from his mother's husband, and sleep was not long delayed in closing Don Sebastian's eyes and making peace between father and son. When Pancorbo had sunk into sleep, Manuel went to look for his mother; he found her weeping.

He kissed her brow and dried her tears, saying: "Courage,
Mother; save your tears for the time when I shall not be with
you."

"My son, I am very miserable."

"You miserable, mother? Are you complaining of God? Has
he not given you a son? Have you not my heart and the blood of
my veins which I will shed for you?" replied the youth warmly.

"Yes, yes, I am wrong; but God will pardon me, as you will
pardon me for forgetting your name. My son, my son; yes, I am
a mother," said Doña Petronila, taking her son by the hand and
making him sit down by her side.

"Poor mother," said Manuel, sighing and contradicting his
own first thought.

"'Poor women' you should say, Manuel. However happy we
may appear, every one of us has some worm that is gnawing at
the soul," said Doña Petronila, a little calmer, fingering the
fringe of her shawl.

"Mother, let us leave complaining and speak calmly of something."

"What do you wish to speak about?"

"I wish to know what our present income is. In this world,
Mother, we cannot take one step forward without knocking
first at the door of the treasure house."

"What! Do you wish to return to college, leaving me shut up
alone, here in this Babylon?"

"Do not rush too far ahead, Mother. I am, as you say, a boy;
but remember that contact with books and men makes us grow
older, giving us experience and teaching us to think. I now consider myself a man," said Manuel proudly.

"Yes, you are a man," said his mother, looking proudly into
the face of her son.

"Well, Mother, I wish to say that, having thought over everything thoroughly, I expect to carry out what I have planned in
respect to your future and mine. Anyone else . . . ."

He was on the verge of uttering harsh words, but the name of
Margarita crossed his mind like a gentle moonbeam reflected on
the surface of a tranquil lake, leaving him silent in mid-phrase
and drawing from him a deep sigh.

"What pleasure I have in hearing you speak in that way, my

son. With reason have Doña Lucia and Don Fernando congratulated me so much on having such a son."

Manuel took new courage from this, and continued: "Mother, I wish to know what our income is, but without counting that of Don Sebastian."

"Our income?" said Doña Petronila, playing unconsciously with the fringe of her shawl. "How can I calculate our income? We have a good piece of ground that produces corn, wheat, barley, beans, and potatoes; some hundreds of sheep, cows, and alpacas; horses that thresh the harvest. I cultivate the ground, change the fleeces and grain to silver, and part of it goes to you at college. Have I managed well?"

Manuel listened to his mother attentively, and when she had finished he kissed her brow, silently and thoughtfully, carrying in his heart his prayer of gratitude and adoration which that holy abnegation and mother-love merited. The account did not leave any round numbers for the plans he had formed, and he asked again timidly: "And you have not saved anything?"

"What! Do you think me a spendthrift? Do I not know that I have a son? Should I not provide for your future? Do I not know that sometime you will wish to settle down for yourself? Well, well! I have saved one half, and here you have, well hidden away, five bags with two thousand shining dollars each. You will not have to endure the shame that some do, of having to marry on nothing."

"Blessed be such mothers as you; they find their happiness in the well-being of their sons! I will take, then, for the foundation of my plans, the ten thousand dollars. I wish to propose a plan to you."

"That is what I said. You wish to leave me."

"Remember, Mother, that a year lost in my studies would perhaps mean the loss of the profession I have chosen, but I shall not go alone, Mother, nor will I go to the same University of San Bernardo."

"It will be, then, as you like; but remember that I am the wife of Don Sebastian, linked to him by gratitude, and you must respect him as much as a true father," replied Doña Petronila, lowering her eyes.

"I will not forget it, Mother. Now let us rest after such a
long day," replied Manuel, kissing his mother good-night.

37
FLEECING
THE
INDIAN

When once Isidro Champi,
the sexton, was shut up in jail,
the door did not open again to give him liberty.

Let us see what happened to his wife that afternoon, when
she went to the house of their friend Escobedo, to ask for help
and advice.

"And so my friend is a prisoner!" exclaimed Escobedo, after
the customary salutations had been exchanged, and the Indian
woman had given him the tidings.

"Yes, my *compadre, wiracocha.* And what shall we do? Will you
help us?" said the woman, in anguish.

Escobedo replied, tapping her lightly on the shoulder: "Ah!
But to ask a favour, you must not come this way with empty
hands, and you who have so many herds, eh?"

"Oh señor! You are right; but I came away from home as if
pursued by spirits, and to-morrow, or later, I will not be ungrateful, like the earth without water."

"Well, well! That is another thing; but to go to speak to the
Judge and Governor, you must tell me what to offer them."

"I shall carry them a chicken!"

"How silly! What are you saying? Do you think that for one
chicken they are going to despatch such a business? My friend is
already in the reports for that row when Yupanqui and the others died," said Escobedo maliciously.

"Oh, señor! What is it you say?" she inquired, wringing her
hands.

"That is just what the trouble is, but by making an effort we will get him out. Tell me, how many cows have you? With some four I think that . . . ."

"With four cows will my Isidro go free?" asked the woman, utterly confounded.

"Surely! We will give one to the Governor; one to the Judge; another to the Sub-Prefect, and the fourth remains for your friend," distributed Escobedo, walking up and down the room, while the poor woman, sunk into a night of doubt and desolation, went over in her mind, one by one, the animals, separating them by their ages and colours, confusing at times the names of her children with those of her favourite calves.

"Well, what are you thinking about, woman? It seems as if you did not care much for your husband," interrupted Escobedo.

"Heaven save me, señor, for not caring for my Isidro. We have grown up together, suffered together! Alas! but . . . ."

"Very well; let us leave all that. I have a great deal to do," said Escobedo, hastening to finish the matter.

"Pardon my foolishness, señor *wiracocha, compadritoy* . . . and yes, we will give you the four cows . . . . They will be heifers . . . . I will go get the two brown ones, one black, and the other spotted, but then you will really let my Isidro out? Now?"

"Yes, soon; of course. I will go right to work, and the day after to-morrow, within three days, everything will be arranged. You see, I have to speak to that Don Fernando Marin; it is he who orders the suit."

On hearing the name of Marin, a ray of light crossed the mind of the poor woman and she said to herself: "Why did I not go to him first? perhaps to-morrow morning it will not be too late."

Taking leave of Escobedo she said, "Go, señor, without delay. I have to take some covering to Isidro, and will tell him that you are going to save us to-day."

"The mouse fell into the trap," said Escobedo to himself, laughing, and went immediately to tell Estéfano how he had arranged matters and that they would divide the four cows between themselves, keeping them exempt from the *embargo* decreed upon the property of Champi, by having them offered as property of Escobedo or Benites.

38

MARGARITA AND MANUEL

The political events that had taken place in the nation's capital must have had a powerful, direct influence on the new scheme of *repartos* of Indian assets developed by the new authorities in Killac and the surrounding province.

The Sub-Prefect was visiting one of the small towns under his jurisdiction, and there he came across a pair of eyes that, situated in a passing female face, pierced him to the marrow of his heart. Being a skilled veteran on Cupid's green battlefields, he was decorated not only with medals but also with wounds, about which he would reminisce with pride in the merry company of men, and as authority had always served faithfully on his side, his honour assumed he would win this skirmish at little cost.

It is worth noting in Killac, and the neighbouring towns where simple customs reign, that people are completely unacquainted with the social evil that undermines the family, prevents the young from marrying, and whose manifestation is the unhappy figure of the fallen woman.

It is the artful seductions that carry the seed of disgrace and misfortune, and behind each one appears nearly always the figure of some potentate, whose meretricious superiority gains the victim, saving the victor.

This time the victim selected by the Colonel to be added to his long list of women martyred by an enterprising man was the graceful young daughter of the man in whose house he received sincere hospitality.

Teodora was a young lady of twenty years, diminutive, looking out serenely from her bright eyes. She wore a pretty dress of pink percale with a pattern of brown foliage, and around her neck a crimson silk kerchief draped like a little cape, fastened in front with an imitation gold clasp set with a mock topaz. Her long tresses, cultivated with great care, were braided and tied at the ends with black ribbons.

Teodora's heart was not a deserted place. She was betrothed

to a young man who was in charge of a neighbouring farm, where he was saving up money for the bridal day, which would be celebrated with town "notables" as sponsors, a long table-cloth spread for three days, and a band of wind instruments.

Teodora was born with an impetuous, mannish character. Once she moved beyond childhood, it was clear that she harboured fiery passions.

She loved her promised husband, and perhaps his absence fired the ardour of her virginal dreams, making her sigh for his daily visits and the loving phrases murmured in the hours of delightful romanticism that are the gateway to the castle of matrimony.

For five days Colonel Paredes remained at the house of Teodora's father, days of continuous feasting and revelry, spurred on by the Sub-Prefect. He devoted his attention to the rustic beauty, whose resistance to his advances only sharpened his interest in her and whetted his desire.

Jugs of wine, kegs of beer, all flowed profusely. The town's two blind fiddlers plied their bows ceaselessly, drawing *mozamalas* and *huaynos* from the resonant strings of the fiddle.

Calling to his side one day the Lieutenant Governor, Paredes said something to him in a low voice. The man responded with a malicious smile and replied in a half-whisper: "Soon we'll catch the rat; but the groundwork must be well laid, my Usía." He went out hurriedly.

Teodora, whose ears had already been wounded by the Colonel's implacable or intimidating words, also called her father to the door, and said with more sorrow than fear, "Father, my heart is in Purgatory."

"But, why, Teoco? You ought to be contented—so many visitors."

"That is just the trouble. The Sub-Prefect has evil intentions concerning me, and if Mariano finds out . . ."

"What are you saying . . . ! The devil . . . ! So that is what Usía has been up to!" said Gaspar, wiping his mouth with his hand.

"Yes, Father; he has told me that, willing or unwilling, he

would carry me off," replied the girl, blushing and lowering her
eyes.

"Hum, hum!" murmured the old man, biting his lips, and
turning around as if to inspect the fields, he added: "The coveted dainty will fall from his lips. Am I already a dead fox?"
Then turning to his daughter he said carelessly; "Go into the
parlour; feign indifference; let them spend a little more of the
money robbed from the people, and—keep your heart for your
husband. I know what I will do afterwards," said Teodora's father, pushing her into the midst of the gathering of guests.

One of the guests who had been watching them said in a low
voice:

"That wily old man! Just look at the way he hands his daughter over to him."

Soon after came the call to supper and all went to the table
where they found laid out, on tablecloths that were not so white
but not really black, a good and plenteous repast. There were
stuffed guinea pigs, piping hot roasts, chicken "nutted" with al-
monds, potatoes cooked in green beans, and the local corn spe-
cialty, *locro colorado*, with fresh cheese.

The Sub-Prefect seated himself by the side of Teodora with an
air of triumph, saying to the company: "I always seek my own comfort, gentlemen, by the side of a good-looking young woman."

"That is the place that belongs to Usía," said several guests,
with a sly allusion.

"And where is your father, Teodora?" inquired someone with
scorn.

"My father? He will be in soon," replied the girl, looking
around.

Two young men were exchanging ribaldries, while another
guest said in a low voice:

"The old man knows when to let business take care of itself! . . . he does not want to intrude."

At that moment Don Gaspar appeared; rubbing his hands
and proceeding to open a bottle of wine, he said merrily,
"Something to quicken the appetite, gentlemen."

"Don Gaspar knows how to do things," said the Sub-Prefect.

So the supper commenced, merry and raucous; Teodora was so perfectly amiable to the Colonel that he imagined the fortress to be already taken.

Manuel, after taking leave of his mother, went to his room, and engulfed in his thoughts, he waited sleepless for the coming of the new day.

When it was time he took up his hat and went to Don Fernando's. He found Margarita alone in the reception room reading. On seeing her, Manuel said to himself: "Now I have a good opportunity to sound her heart, and declare my affection."

And going over to the girl and giving her a hug, he said:

"How all alone and how beautiful I find you, Margarita!"

"Manuel, how are you?" replied the girl, laying down the book she had been reading.

"Lovely Margarita; it is the first time I have the opportunity of speaking to you alone; perhaps the moments will be short, for I came to see Don Fernando—therefore I beg you to listen to me, my Margarita!" said Manuel, taking the girl's hand and looking at her tenderly.

"Why, Manuel, how strange you are," said she.

"Do not call me strange, Margarita; you are the soul of my soul, and ever since I have known you I have given you my heart and . . . I wish to be worthy of you!" said Manuel, employing the last phrase because of the fear he had that Margarita would repulse him, who was the son of he who had sacrificed Marcela—an idea which could not exist in the girl of to-day, but might, perhaps, in the woman of to-morrow.

The orphan remained mute, blushing like the poppy. There are occasions in which silence reveals more than words.

Manuel caressed the diminutive hand that was lost in his.

Manuel was drunk with love contemplating the beautiful young girl, and spoke to her again:

"Speak, Margarita! You are still a child, but you know how I love you! Remember that by the side of your blessed mother I asked to be your brother; to-day . . . ."

"Yes, Manuel, I see you in my joys and in my sorrows; you will be my brother," replied the girl.

But Manuel responded quickly: "No, my angel! 'Brother' is
little, and I love you much; I wish to be your husband."

"My husband?" asked Margarita in astonishment, and in that
moment the veil of her childlike imaginings was withdrawn
from her eyes, shaking her entire organism, plunging into her
heart a dart dipped in the drug of youth that, in the sublime
slumber of hearts in love, would make her dream of that world
of poetry, fears and trust, laughter and tears, light and shadow,
wherein dwells the chastity of a virgin.

Margarita knew from that she was a woman—knew she
loved.

Impressions were streaming through Manuel's mind at the
speed of thought, although his emotions were unlike Margarita's, since his soul had already lost the virginity that only
lasts as long as one remains ignorant of the true mysteries of life.

Manuel loved with purpose, Margarita only with feeling.

Manuel's first impulse was to seal with his lips the word
"husband," pronounced by the lips of the adored woman, but
reflection reined in the material being just as the bridle holds
back the charging steed, and he only said:

"Yes, your husband!" and Manuel kissed Margarita's brow.
The kiss was not a burning ember upon the fresh petal of the
lily; yet it left an indelible trace.

Margarita felt an unknown current course through her veins;
her cheeks were tinged with red, and she ran out of the room,
saying to Manuel:

"I will call my godfather." And she went to Lucia's room,
pausing instinctively in the hallway, to calm her agitation.

Manuel remained like one with his soul swept away; his state
was nothing like a bodily dream, and he was aroused from his
trance only by the calm voice of Don Fernando.

Manuel was enslaved to a woman.

A woman, who only constitutes:

To the doctor, the vehicle of reproduction.

To the botanist, a light plant.

To the fat man, a good cook.

To Vice: pleasure, sensation.

To Virtue: a mother.

To a noble, loving heart: soul of my soul!

No one should set to quibbling over the precision of these definitions, taken, no doubt, from some good source; but the truth is that the last one belongs by all rights to Manuel; so Manuel, watching Margarita leave, sent her off with a parting sigh that said: Soul of my soul!

39
DOUBTS, FEARS, AND HOPES

When Lucia found herself alone with Margarita, after Don Fernando had gone in to see Manuel, she said to her: "How happy you will be, Margarita, when you hear what I have to tell you. You and Rosalia will not take your journey to Lima alone."

"Who else is going?" asked the girl quickly.

"Don Fernando and I, all the family."

"All of us. How glorious! And Manuel, will he go also?" asked Margarita.

Lucia fixed her eyes upon Margarita to measure the impression her reply would cause, and said: "Manuel will not go; he has his parents here."

A short silence ensued. Margarita's eyes filled with tears which in vain she tried to hide, saying: "What a beautiful city Lima must be."

"It is the most beautiful city in Perú. But why do you weep, Margarita?" said Lucia, drawing the girl to her side. "My dear, I notice that you are much inclined to Manuel, and now I understand that this young man has impressed your girl's heart, and I begin to fear that to-morrow your woman's heart will also belong to him."

"It is that Manuel is so good; I have never seen him do anything wrong," said the girl timidly.

"Exactly, my dear! His kindness has made me fall into a net

which it is necessary to cut in order to free you. You cannot love
the son of the man who sacrificed your parents. Oh! it horrifies
me! Poor Manuel!" Lucia, overcome by emotion, could not continue. Fear and doubt besieged her heart, and their tones crept
into her voice. Through her mind flashed, one after another,
thoughts that tortured her soul, and inwardly she asked herself:

"Have I committed an indiscretion when I spoke to my goddaughter of love? I have left Manuel eternally branded, and
Margarita will forever see him as the son of her parents' execu-
tioners . . . . And Manuel . . . ! Ah . . . ! The heart is full of
abysses . . . a tangle of mysteries . . . the human heart!"

Poor Margarita! She remained mute and trembling, like a
white lily upon whose stalk the nightingale has attempted to
alight without folding its wings. After the interview which she
had just had with Manuel, this declaration of Lucia's was cruel,
disturbing her soul, blighting at birth the flowers of hope of two
hearts united together by the ties that constitute human felicity—of two hearts that loved each other.

At last Lucia recovered her serenity, and cutting off the
thread of her former conversation, said to Margarita: "My dear,
be careful to have your trunk ready for Wednesday, and do not
forget your sister's things; you are older and should help her."

"I will see about it now," replied the girl as she left the room.

"Poor Manuel!" continued Lucia to herself when alone.

"He is so full of talent, so gifted with noble aspirations!
There's no doubt he loves Margarita, but between them there
stretches an abyss! . . . but . . . it's true, in the course of living, the
heart's mysteries reveal to us an unfathomable world, the most
poetic part of love. Is there any flame comparable to that which
fuels impossible loves? Is there any urge like that which spurs
the lover on in his drive to possess the beloved object, breaking
bonds, crossing mountain ranges bristling with thorns that tear
at the feet; scaling steep mountains where the snow of impossible longings, melted by the sun of love, has formed floods
of tears?

"Heroes of suffering, poor souls cast out of the Paradise of
Bliss, the world does not understand you! Burnt offerings on the
altars of misfortune, perhaps generous souls will offer you the

incense of their sympathy, and you will not cease to love, amidst your pain and grief!"

Lucia fell back upon the sofa as she came to the end of her soliloquy, drawing her right hand across her forehead, which was bathed in copious perspiration that rolled over her cheeks, which were burning with the hue of May poppies. Then, clasping her hands and wringing them as if she would throw all her fingers out of joint, she asked herself:

"What shall I do, then? My situation is as difficult and dramatic as Manuel and Margarita's; if they are living out a first love, their love will blossom into those sighs that, laden with the scent of virginal love, waft from a heart heavy with longing for the loved one . . . . Perhaps if it were brought into the open . . . . Oh . . . ! But my Fernando will help me resolve my confusion; we will share our ideas, and together reach the light. I can never forget that Marcela died leaving me the two pieces of her heart!"

Lucia was right; she would share with Don Fernando her doubts, fears, and hopes, brushing aside the shadows that darkened the moment; Manuel could share with his mother, with the noblest of hearts, the sorrows that afflicted his own heart; he could take refuge in the maternal lap and cry his man's tears today, just as yesterday she wiped away his childish weeping.

But Margarita?

Poor orphan, bird without a nest, she would have to seek the shade of a tree not her own, and under its branches sing the idyll of her soul, united to another; she would have to hide her own thoughts, and smile with her lips and weep with her heart.

Lucia was, for Margarita, the best of women; but Lucia was not her mother!

40
TEODORA'S
ESCAPE

Let us journey for a moment in search of Colonel Paredes, whom we last saw taking a seat by Teodora.

The meal was festive and abundant, and it was already night when it was finished. The company adjourned to the parlour for a lively round of the *zapateo* and the handkerchief dance.

Don Gaspar called his daughter to his side, and said softly: "Follow me." Both slipped out quietly, going to a hedge nearby where they found three horses saddled, one of them prepared for a woman.

"Where are we going, Father?" asked Teodora.

"To Killac—to the house of my friend Doña Petronila who, as you know, is the right kind of a lady, and by whose side you will be as safe as the holy vessel on the altar," replied Don Gaspar hurrying on.

"Good, and it is well that Sebastian is not Governor anymore, so we will be in peace until my Mariano comes," said Teodora, keeping close to her father's side. A dark object appeared at that moment. "Anselmo!" called Don Gaspar.

"Señor!" replied the shadow, and the three continued their march.

When they reached the horses, Teodora was given a lift up by the men, and mounted, with the agility of a country girl, her horse, named El Chollopoccochi, no doubt because it was black with white legs.

Don Gaspar and Anselmo, who was a confidential servant of the house, followed.

Don Gaspar then said to an Indian who was waiting: "Return to the house; keep everything in order, have the tea ready, and if we are missed you know what to do, eh?"

"Yes, señor," replied the Indian, turning away.

Three lashes sounded simultaneously and the three horses sprang forward like a flash in the darkness of the night.

The old man rode on, lost in meditation, as the brain works on without ceasing, and thought does not submit to the quietude of the body.

"Father! Let us slacken our pace a little," called Teodora, reining in her horse.

"What! Are you fatigued so soon?"

"I am not fatigued! What an idea; but I have thought of something."

"Speak then," replied her father, holding in his horse.

"It would be better that you should return from here. You will arrive home in half an hour; your presence will quiet all suspicion, and they will go on a while longer without missing me—and you will make many excuses."

"And you, will you go alone?" asked Don Gaspar, coughing several times.

"I do not run any risk whatever in going with Anselmo; my horse is gentle and knows the road well; the distance is short and the moon will soon rise—and, above all, if it has occurred to them to look for us if they find out about our journey, there is no doubt they will follow or perhaps overtake us, and they have been drinking . . . ."

"Very true, Teodora; you speak like a prayer book," he said interrupting her, stopping his horse, and he added with a malicious smile, "Women are born to invent these little deceptions."

Don Gaspar coughed again, violently.

"There! You have taken cold already. Go back at once, and if anyone should come looking for us, by your return they will lose the track."

"All right, and before I declare where you are, they may skin me," replied Don Gaspar.

"Anselmo! Anselmo!" he shouted. The servant came up and received his instructions.

"Good-bye, daughter! Within four days I will go to look for you."

"Good-bye, Father! Cover up your mouth—your cough is bad."

"Knock cautiously when you arrive and tell my friend Petronila everything. The frog knows in what water it can swim."

"Yes, I will tell her everything."

"Anselmo, take care of my daughter." So saying, Don Gaspar turned his horse and galloped towards home.

It would be somewhere about eleven o'clock that night when Teodora and Anselmo arrived at the house of Doña Petronila. They knocked loudly, and at the noise four or five dogs began to bark furiously, while a sleepy voice inquired shortly: "Who is it?"

"I come from Don Gaspar Sierra to deliver to Doña Petronila a pledge which he sends her."

No further explanations were asked; the door opened and
Teodora passed in and was received by the mother of Manuel
with her proverbial kindness.

Don Gaspar had not gone two miles from the place where he
left Teodora, when he began to distinguish the shouting and
tramping of people on horseback. In a few minutes he could see
clearly they were the followers of the Sub-Prefect.

"Yes! How well Teoco guessed what would happen. Women
are witches! And the best of it is that we men, all of us, let ourselves be bewitched by them, eyes and ears," said Don Gaspar to
himself, following on at an even pace.

41
THE
PURSUIT

Not long after Teodora's flight,
she was missed by the company.
The Lieutenant Governor was the first to give the notice.

"The old man is the one to blame, Colonel," he said, "for to
all appearance the girl was ready enough to please you."

"Do they think to fool me that way—me? I will not consent;
never. No, señor, I will not consent, by the word of a soldier,"
declared Paredes, pacing excitedly up and down the room.

"Come on, friends, let us look for her," proposed the Lieutenant, catching up a lighted candle.

"Yes, señor, I will hunt out any girl from the depths of the
earth. Yes, señor!" shouted the Sub-Prefect with fury, while his
officious followers went out to search the entire house, ques-
tioning and cross-questioning all the servants, although all answered alike: "They have gone out into the street."

"Did they go out on foot?"

"No, señor, they went on horseback."

"Usía, we will follow them," was shouted in chorus, "there is only one road."

"To the work, then, friends; to the one who brings me the girl . . . ."

"I swear that I will be the fortunate one," interrupted the Lieutenant. The commission was named and those designated went after their horses. The wrath of the Sub-Prefect was ready to break out anew. He said to himself: "The old man! If they would bring him to me now, I would shoot him without the form of a council of war! One is not put in a place of authority for nothing! But the boys are active and . . . I will rest a moment." So saying he threw himself down on a bed in a corner of the room and soon began to doze.

In a few minutes he heard the galloping of horses, and, opening his eyes, Don Bruno Paredes said between his teeth: "They have started already. Yes, señor, very soon I shall be pleased, thanks to the activity of my subordinates. These boys are worth a mine of silver."

A few moments after the departure of the men in search of Teodora, a message arrived, brought by a *chasqui,* an Indian runner in government service, who had made his way on foot through the steep and sinuous routes from the capital to Killac, covering ground at a prodigious rate. This *chasqui* bore a sheet sealed with red wax, with the seal of the Republic, on which could be read: "Official—Urgent—Colonel Don Bruno Paredes."

When this was put in the hands of the Colonel he began to read it as he was, half-reclining on the bed; but no sooner had he gathered the meaning of the first few lines than he sprang to his feet as if thrown up by some electric force. He turned pale, then all the blood seemed to rush to his head; he remained standing a moment as if in suspense, then threw the paper on the bed exclaiming: "Ho! ho! this has a bad look. The best thing for me to do is to make myself safe, yes, señor!" and, raising his voice, began to shout for the servants, who came running from different directions.

"My horse! Quick, quick!!"

Don Bruno mounted in haste, and, followed by three of his suite, galloped away in the direction of the city. "The most

prudent plan is to escape at once. In the city I will find some
hiding-place until the political tempest calms down," he muttered to himself.

The people who went in search of Teodora met Don Gaspar
jogging along on his pony and surrounded him, whilst the Lieutenant began: "Well, old man! This is a fine trick you have
played on us! Where is the girl Teodora?"

"How?" replied Don Gaspar, feigning anxiety. "You are
looking for my daughter? What! Did I not leave her with you
all? Happily she is honest, and . . . she will be there, come on,"
applying the whip to his horse that began to jump about briskly.

"Softly, softly!!" observed several, taking hold of the bridle,
and the Lieutenant added: "Come on then, but if you do not deliver up the girl . . . ."

"She cannot have gone away; there has not been time to go to
any town and return," said one.

"And if you did not go away with Teodora, Don Gaspar,
what are you doing about here?" asked the Lieutenant.

"O, go along with you! You do not seem to belong about
here; you must have come from Lima with a cane and stiff
collar! I have come from making the circuit of the pastures
and looking after the sheep," observed Don Gaspar with much
formality.

"Let us refresh ourselves a little," said one.

They stopped, and the leader, taking out a bottle, passed it to
each one. This operation was repeated several times during the
return journey.

They found everything quiet at the house of Don Gaspar.
The *pongos* in the yard were sleeping so soundly that it required
some vigorous shaking to arouse them.

"Where is the Señor Sub-Prefect?"

"The Señor Sub-Prefect has gone away on horseback,"
replied one of the *pongos.*

"Without doubt we have been absent a long time and he has
gone in search of us," observed one.

They entered the parlour, and as Don Gaspar lighted the
candle that was found near the bed, the first thing he saw was

the sheet of paper which had made Colonel Bruno Paredes turn tail and run. They all gathered round to read it together, and when they had, Teodora's father said:

"So our Sub-Prefect has run away."

"He was an idiot, anyway, that National Guard Colonel!" said the Lieutenant Governor.

"A sham!"

"A coward!" added another.

"A crook, an embezzler!" said yet another.

"A coward! A deserter!" were the judgments of another.

"An ex-authority," explained Don Gaspar laughing, like one who has lived long and heard much.

Taking up a guitar from the corner, he began to strum, singing in his rheumy voice:

> Bird on the wing
> Down by the sea
> Aren't you afraid
> With no safe place to be?

To the strains of this odd little ditty harmony was restored between the pursuers and the pursued; now let us return to Killac, where our protagonists await us.

42
MANUEL'S
BIRTH
VEILED

Don Fernando found Manuel still absorbed in the reflections caused by the sudden departure of Margarita.

"How are you, Manuel?" he said, giving his hand to his visitor.

"Excuse my visit, Don Fernando; it is not the proper hour, but in these cases urgency of business is the passport," replied Manuel.

"There is no call for ceremony, Manuel. You know that I am your friend and that is sufficient," said Don Fernando, drawing forward a chair for the young man.

"I know it so well that without your friendship I think I should have become insane. My position before you, so difficult since the assault; the many contradictory events that have taken place since my arrival here, where the people in authority pay no attention either to law or religion; and other things that occupy my thoughts—these all weigh upon me."

"True, Manuel; the present state of this small place horrifies me. Also I have heard some even more troubling news from the city."

"Is it a personal matter?"

"No, it is of general concern. I have heard of the sad end of Father Pascual, that unfortunate man from whom we heard such words of sorrow, longing for the healthy influence that, in the future, priests will enjoy in the bosom of the family."

"He is dead?"

"Yes. He was thrown from his horse, found by some charitable people and taken to the convent where he was cared for by the monks. They say that on taking a glass of water he died immediately. The doctors think his death was caused by a sudden rush of blood to the brain. Poor man, let him rest in peace."

"Then there is even worse news that makes me wonder . . . ."

"Do you mean that which we already heard at home? Concerning the political storm unleashed in the nation's capital, and stirred up as the result of a horrifying delirium?"

"Exactly, my friend! but . . . it is one of those crises that are terrible right at the outset, because extreme situations bring on violent measures. Later, less so. I have faith in the government of your namesake, Manuel," said Don Fernando, rising from his seat.

"I, too, have faith, Don Fernando, because Don Manuel Pardo is a man a cut above . . . but . . . changing the topic a little—I find it impossible to live in this town, governed, as it is, so tyrannically, by persons who presume so much upon a little authority. Then, if I wish to finish my studies and be received as a lawyer, I must go away; but I cannot decide to leave my mother in this den of wolves."

"Well, my friend, I have just decided this grave matter in the same way. Within a few days I leave with my family."

"You, Don Fernando!" interrupted the young man in surprise.

"Yes; I have arranged to transfer my shares in the mines and other property to some Jews who give me twenty per cent, and so I go satisfied."

"And where are you going?"

"To the capital. In Lima I presume that the home will be protected, and the authorities will know how to fulfil their mission. I would like to do something to liberate the poor sexton before I go."

"I am with you heart and soul, Don Fernando. We will both do everything possible for that poor Indian. Now it seems that destiny smiles upon me. I have come to speak to you about something relative to my projects."

"I will listen with pleasure."

"As I said, I desire to take my mother away from here. I have taken all the steps necessary for taking her away, under the pretext of a visit to Lima, and once there, there will be no boat to return in!"

"Perfectly right, and Don Sebastian?" inquired Señor Marin with curiosity.

"You know that the true centre of light and warmth in the house is the mother; after my mother I would assist Don Sebastian, whose future is also one of the saddest here . . . ah, Don Fernando, you cannot guess all the oppressive acts I endure for love of my mother."

"Don Manuel, your manner of expressing yourself regarding your father has attracted my attention for some time," said Don Fernando, inspiring by the tone of his voice a certain confidence in the young man.

"I presumed so, Señor Marin. My birth is hidden by a mysterious veil and if, sometime, my hand draws it aside, it will be before you who are a gentleman and my best friend."

Don Fernando had learned what he needed, for the mutual impressions of Manuel and Margarita had not passed unperceived by him. Manuel was not, could not be, the son of Sebastian Pancorbo.

"Who can be his father?" he asked himself. "I might question him, exact his confidence as from friend to friend, obtain
the secret and have the field to myself. But I ought to respect the
prudent reserve of the young man; the occasion will come."

Turning to Manuel he said: "I believe myself to be worthy of
your confidence. But let us return to your petition."

"I desire that you should help me send some funds to Lima
and deposit them in some good commercial house."

"With the greatest pleasure. We can work through some of
the banks, the Providence, the London, the Mexican, any one
which you select."

"Let it be the London."

"Very well. How much do you wish me to remit?"

"For the present some ten thousand dollars. Later, much
more, for I intend to sell all the property here."

"It shall be done. This afternoon you can pass the money
into Salas, and to-morrow you shall have your papers. And now,
allow me to congratulate you on your resolution, very well
planned. You will be a man useful to your country like many others who have gone from the provinces to the capital. You will be
an honour to your family, I assure you," said Don Fernando.

Manuel bowed his appreciation of these remarks, and was
going to declare to Don Fernando that the inspiration to all his
efforts was the thought of Margarita, but some feeling kept him
from doing so.

"Your mother must have suffered a great deal."

"Oh, cruelly! A woman's heart is as sensitive as an angel's.
My poor mother!" Then taking another thought he added: "Do
you know what happened last night to complicate matters still
further?"

"What happened?"

"There came to us from the neighbouring town of Saucedo a
young woman, who is now sheltered in our house from the per-
secutions of the Sub-Prefect Paredes."

"The girl should have paid some tax or fiscal income?"

"Nothing of the kind. The Colonel was pleased with her
youthful beauty and wished to make her his without other bene-
diction than his own dictatorial will!"

"And so?"

"She ran away from home, aided by her father, to take shelter with my mother."

"So then, in these parts of the world, the victims who escape the hands of the priests fall into the power of the authorities!"

"As you see," replied Manuel.

"This horrifies me. And if we fix our eyes on the Indians, the heart grows desperate before the oppression which they endure from the priests and the *caciques!*"

"Ah, Señor Fernando, these things cannot fail to afflict an honourable man coming from other parts, who sees and feels. When I write my graduating discourse I intend to prove, with all these facts, the necessity of ecclesiastical marriage—that is, of the priests."

"You will touch upon a fact of vital importance, a point which social progress must make clear before many years have elapsed."

"That is my conviction also, Don Fernando."

"And what can you tell me of the authorities who come to govern these out-of-the-way parts of the rich and wide Perú?" asked Don Fernando.

"Ah, my friend! They seek employment, salary, and comfort without having taken notice of the words of Epaminondas: 'It is the *man* who dignifies destiny.'"

"It is because everything goes by favour," replied Don Fernando, taking out a box of matches and lighting the cigar that he had been holding at the ready for some time.

"Could you tell me, Don Fernando, what has become of the complaint you filed concerning the attack on your house?" asked Manuel, seizing upon a brief lapse in the conversation to introduce the topic; as he inquired, a bright crimson tinged his cheeks.

"The complaint . . . I scarcely know what to tell you, my friend . . . just yesterday I inquired about it when I learned that they had jailed the sexton, whom I believe is entirely innocent; are you interested?" answered Don Fernando, exhaling a cloud of smoke.

"A great deal, Don Fernando! We have agreed to do all we can to free the sexton, whose name I do not know, and then as one day . . . she will learn of them in a different light . . . ."

"Ah! What a tragedy, the way the poor girl's parents died!"

"What wouldn't I give if the entire story could be revealed to
your worthy goddaughter! Margarita! And Margarita . . . ."

Manuel was on the verge of laying bare his entire heart, when
Doña Petronila appeared in the door accompanied by Teodora,
whom she presented with manifest kindness and respect.

43
THE HIDE,
THEN THE FLESH

Let us retrace our steps a moment. Martina, the wife of Isidro
Champi, as soon as she left the house of Escobedo, after sacrificing the four cows to the avarice of her friend, frightened at
the news that the imprisonment of her husband was really because of the ringing of the bells at the time of the attack, went
running to her house, took the warm *poncho* for Isidro, and hurried to the jail.

The jailor gave her free entrance; when she saw her husband
she began to cry like a crazy woman: "Isidro! Isidrocha! Where
do I see you? Alas, alas! Your heart and mine are clean from robbery and death! Alas, alas!"

"Patience, Martina; keep your tears and pray to the Virgin,"
replied Isidro, trying to calm his wife who, drying her eyes with
the border of the *poncho*, replied: "Do you know, Isidro, that I
have been to see our friend Escobedo, and he says that he will
soon set you free."

"He has said so?"

"Yes, and I have already paid him."

"What have you paid him? Has he asked for money?"

"No. He says they have arrested you because of the bell-ringing that night of the assault on the house of Don Fernando—and so many deaths there were! That *wiracocha*—they say—has money and will prosecute us," said the woman, crossing herself as she thought of the dead.

"And that was what Estéfano said also," replied Isidro; and going back to his first question, for he knew full well the power and customs of the notables of the place, he said: "But what did you pay? Tell me plainly."

"Isidrocha! Do not be angry; you are getting as bitter as the bark of the *molle*."

"Come, Martina, have you come to torture me like the worm that gnaws at the heart of the sheep? Speak, or else go and leave me alone—I do not know why you will not tell me what you paid."

"Well, Isidro, I have given to our friend what he asked, because you were in prison; because I am your dove-mate; because I must save you although it be at the cost of my life. Do not be angry, Isidro! I have given him the two chestnuts, the black, and the spotted one," enumerated Martina, drawing nearer her husband.

"Ay, four heifers!" exclaimed the Indian, lifting up his hands and giving such a deep sigh that we do not know whether it lifted one weight from his heart, or left one in place of another.

"Yes. He wished that I should give him the cows, and it was like taking the grass out by the roots that I could get the 'yes' from him for the cows, for one has to go to the Governor, one to the Sub-Prefect, one to the Judge, and one to our friend."

The Indian listened in silence to this relation, inclining his head gloomily without daring to say anything to Martina, who, after waiting some moments, went away to her children, drying new tears, her heart divided between the prison and her cabin.

In the meantime, Escobedo, meeting Estéfano, said to him: "Comrade, everything is sure; the Indian Isidro gave up the four cows. The woman came crying and I told her the case was serious, because the imprisonment was for the bell-ringing."

"And what then?"

"She offered me hens! What do you think of that?"

"But she gave up the cows?"

"Yes. Now, how shall we divide them?"

"We will give one to the Sub-Prefect—it is best to go directly to the saint—and the remaining three for . . . no names,"
said Benites.

"Good, and the Indian, shall he go out or not?"

"It would not suit us for him to go out just now; we will
humbug him for a month or so, then the sentence will be given,
for first comes the hide, then the flesh, my son," argued Benites.

"That is very true; one is before two. And the *embargo?*"

"The distress warrant will come in due form, and then we
will take out at least four cows more, of course."

"You talk like a book, Estéfano; it is not strange that everyone makes you their Secretary," added Escobedo, rubbing his
hands.

"And why should one study in the school of the lash, except
to dictate to others, earn a living, and be a public man—a man
of respect," replied Estéfano with emphasis, wiping his mouth
on a coarse handkerchief.

"When will the warrant be made?"

"It can be done within ten days, and now an idea occurs to
me. You must not go to the seizure, then we can make the Indian believe that you, being his friend, have interested yourself
in taking care of the herds; for if they are entrusted with someone else, he will carry them away!"

"Magnificent! But what will Don Hilarión say?"

"Oh, the old man never even reads what I write; he says
'amen' to everything since his grandfather was a priest."

"That is no way to talk. And Don Sebastian?"

"Don Sebastian will say: 'Really, that seems to me to be
right,'" said Estéfano, laughing boisterously. His brain harboured
a fully laid plan to exploit the innocence of Isidro Champi, with
the help of Escobedo, who was his *compadre*, having been godfather at the baptism of the sexton's second son.

"Very good! And now that we have everything clearly arranged,
what do you say to something to moisten our tongues?"

"Absolutely, *compadrito;* we will have a glass or two at La
Quiquijaneña's place, or maybe La Rufa," answered Estéfano,
accepting his friend's suggestion and adjusting his hat brim.

44
A HEROINE OF LOVE

Teodora was in the full bloom of youth, as we have already described her to you while visiting her home; she possessed such an abundant head of long hair that if she let it loose, it would have covered her back like a spreading mantle of undulating vapour. Her entire person was so engaging and attractive, with that sweet expression that steals one's heart away, that when Don Fernando saw her, he could almost excuse the Sub-Prefect his conduct. He invited the new arrivals to sit down, and called from the door, "Lucia, Lucia!" throwing away the butt of the cigar he had been smoking.

Meanwhile Doña Petronila said softly to her son: "I have found you out, my boy. I know now."

"Mother!" said Manuel, like a boy asking a pardon.

Don Fernando addressed himself to Teodora: "Señorita, have you arrived recently?"

"Yes, Señor; I have come from Saucedo and have been here only a few hours."

Lucia entered, saluting both ladies cordially.

Doña Petronila, loosening her shawl, said frankly: "What do you think of that harpy, Colonel Paredes, who, after planting the seeds of discord in my family, went to the house of my friend Don Gaspar Sierra to rob him of his daughter?" indicating Teodora.

"Mother!" said Manuel timidly.

"Why should I not speak plainly? Don Fernando and Doña Lucia know all about these things," said Doña Petronila, and she gave a full account of what had occurred at Saucedo, to which both husband and wife listened attentively.

Teodora's cheeks were like two cherries, and she remained with her eyes fixed upon the floor, without courage to raise them to the kind faces about her. It was one of the most trying moments of her life. She drew her feet up under the chair and wrung her hands hidden under her cashmere shawl.

Manuel smiled from time to time. Lucia played with the edging of her fine handkerchief, bunching it up and then letting it

"So this young lady is a heroine of love for her betrothed?"
said Don Fernando.

"But that is marvellous of her! All women should be so faithful to love," expounded Lucia.

"What a joy to see such strength of love! I envy Mariano!"
added Manuel.

"I like your way of treating the Sub-Prefect," said Don Fernando, rising from his chair and shaking Teodora's hand. "It
seems to me these towns are becoming worse every day. Everyone is out for personal gain and no one corrects the bad or stim-
ulates the good; but it is surprising that women and men are
nothing alike in their behaviour."

"If the women were bad, too, this would be a hell!" said
Lucia, putting her handkerchief back in her pocket.

Then Don Fernando said to Doña Petronila, "You ought to
save your husband and encourage your son, who is a thorough
gentleman."

Lucia added: "True, my friend; this is no longer any place for
us; we must take flight to other and serener regions. We shall
leave here very soon."

"You are going away?"

"Yes; we have resolved to do so very soon."

"What sad news I have come to hear," said Doña Petronila,
to whom Manuel turned to say: "Now it only remains for you
to decide also, Mother, and we shall all be contented."

"Margarita, come in," said Lucia, seeing the girl pass the
door.

Lucia wished to see what impression Margarita would make
upon Doña Petronila.

"Let me present to you my godchild, Margarita," said Lucia,
taking the girl by the hand and turning to the mother of Manuel
and to Teodora.

"What a beautiful young lady!"

"Winning and good-natured."

So said Doña Petronila and Teodora.

"Margarita! Is it not true that she wears her flower-name well?" added Manuel when his mother embraced the orphan with showers of caresses and words of praise, which sounded like celestial music in the ears of the young man.

To interrupt this peaceful scene came a woman, terror-stricken and weeping, who from the door cried between her sobs: "Señor Fernando, charity for the Virgin's sake."

"Who is that unhappy woman?" inquired Don Fernando in surprise.

"It is Martina, wife of Champí," replied Doña Petronila.

Lucia, covering her face with her hands, said to herself: "Marcela! Marcela! She looks as if she might be her sister."

Turning to the woman, Don Fernando asked: "Who are you and what do you want?"

"I am the wife of Isidro Champí, the sexton." The last phrase tore the veil away completely.

"Don Fernando and Manuel exchanged glances, and the former said: "Ah yes! I know; your husband is a prisoner, is he not?"

"Yes, *wiracocha;* and they have just taken away our animals also."

"Who has taken them?"

"The authorities, señor."

"But who are these authorities?"

"The Judge and the Governor. *Wiracochay,* mercy!" cried Martina, kneeling at the feet of Don Fernando.

"Rise, and be calm!" said Don Fernando, giving Martina his hand.

"Yes, yes; we will save you. Everything will be arranged," added Manuel.

"You do not prosecute us, then?" she asked Señor Marin.

"No, no, my good woman, no!"

"You will save us then, will take Isidro out of prison and our animals from the *embargo?*"

"Yes, yes, we will defend you."

"Cruel, heartless," repeated all, and Martina, without other promises than those of Don Fernando, went out full of the hopes which her loving wifely heart wished to carry without delay to her imprisoned husband.

45
ONE
AGAINST
FIVE
THOUSAND

The change in authority was effected peacefully in the province. The new Sub-Prefect directed the customary circulars to the different functionaries under his supervision, invoking law, justice, and equity.

Don Gaspar came over to Killac to relate to his daughter all that had occurred in Saucedo since her flight, to thank Doña Petronila for her hospitality, and to accompany his daughter back to his house to take up anew her tranquil country life until the day her marriage with the honest Mariano should come.

No one knew anything about the stopping-place of Colonel Paredes, for after riding a few miles he dismissed his escort and went on alone to find a safe refuge. It was discovered long after that he had a good fortune, well secured, the fruit of many well-laid schemes—lawful when considered according to the old adage "Might makes right."

Don Sebastian, seeing his new plans suddenly frustrated, grew peevish and gloomy; smiting his breast he would cry: "Really, my wife and Manuel knew what they were about. I am sorry I did not follow their advice."

Such a confession was a new support to Manuel, who soon found his opinions respected and obeyed. As for Manuel, he had no sleep that night; he sat with a pencil in his hand, marking down and erasing numbers on a piece of paper, and pacing his bedroom swiftly, occasionally stopping to note something down or to rest a little on the sofa.

"Why," he would soliloquize, "am I so anxious to leave the place where I was born, when it is man's natural impulse to love and seek the upbuilding of the place where he first saw the light? Why do I not aspire to live here where Margarita was born, and where by her side sprang up, beautiful and bright, the flower of my love? Ah, this seeming contradiction is explained and justified by cruel experiences. Those places where one cannot count upon any guarantee for property or family soon become uninhabited; all who can dispose of sufficient means to do so emigrate to a more civilised country, and when one finds himself in a situation like mine—alone against two, one against five thousand—there is no remedy but to fly and seek in other parts tranquility for my friends, and the eternal spring of my own heart. Margarita mine, you would become hardened and benumbed by the winter of deceit and crime in this place where all good sentiments are killed by the frosts of abuse and bad example. In another clime you will live fresh and beautiful, where your soul will be understood and your beauty admired; you will be the sun that will give me warmth and life under the shade of a strange tree!"

The mind of Doña Petronila's son was interwoven with a tangle of live wires, bearing along a swarm of illusions sustained in his heart by two active forces: nobility of sentiment and purity of passion. He paced around the room a few times, distracted and absorbed in his thoughts, and took out a cigar kept in a little rubber case. Manuel very seldom smoked. Tobacco, far from being a vice in his case, was a pastime. He readied the cigar, and after lighting it from the flame of a wax candle, drawing upon it three times, and exhaling smoke out of his mouth and nose, he said: "Yes! They leave soon . . . I will go find them, though it be to the ends of the earth! . . . and far from Killac, far from the scene of the tragic events of the fifth of August, I will lay my heart bare to Don Fernando, ask for Margarita's hand, and once accepted, we will set the marriage date, and I will throw myself into my studies, and begin the career I have embraced. Yes! My mind is set on it! . . . I will entrust Don Fernando, Lucia, and Margarita with the secret of my birth, and by taking them into my confidence, will assure my happiness, but . . . first I must speak with my generous mother; I would never do anything to cast the slightest blight on her honour. Mother! Beloved mother . . . ! Fate sent me to your womb, and then . . . . My presence was a torture in your life, and so was the

hard-headed man who became my stepfather . . . ! And now that
I feel I am a man, why cannot all the warmth of my affections
be for you alone? Margarita . . . !!"

The first ray of the breaking dawn, peaceful and serene, came
through the cracks in the door and window of Manuel's bedroom. He had gone from one day to the next without closing
his eyes, sleepless, torn between love and duty.

46
FERNANDO ENLIGHTENS LUCIA

The object of Doña Petronila's
visit to Señor Marin was not
simply to introduce Teodora and relate the news from Saucedo,
but also to obtain from Don Fernando some recommendation
to the new authority. Therefore, as soon as Martina Champi
had gone, she said: "I have come to trouble you, Don Fernando,
with a petition."

"It will never be a trouble, Doña Petronila."

"They tell me that you are a friend of the new Sub-Prefect."

"I am acquainted with him, it is true, but very slightly. But
what can I do for you?"

"I wish a letter of recommendation for Teodora and her father. After what they have passed through, the poor things will
be trembling for fear that other bad people, like that Colonel,
will be going there."

"I am sorry that I am not able to serve you myself, but will
seek the influence of some friend."

"Is not Salas a relative of the new Sub-Prefect?" suggested
Lucia.

"Yes, but it is not of him I am thinking, but of Guzmán, because Guzmán will help me to work for Isidro Champi."

"And you also, Doña Petronila, for your part see how Don

Sebastian can arrange the matter of the poor Indian," recommended Lucia.

"That will be my charge," replied Doña Petronila, as she took leave and retired with Teodora and Manuel, to whom Don Fernando said: "We will see each other again soon to arrange about Champi."

Margarita, who went inside the house looking for Rosalia, breathed freer away from her godmother; ever since she had confided in her and Manuel had spoken the way he had, Lucia had been looking at Margarita with close attention.

The air that solitude provides to those hearts that suffer in the asphyxia of pain is imbued with melancholy, and seems to be warmed by the balsam of consolation.

Love is like a plant.

Rooted in fertile, exuberant, rich soil, it grows with surprising speed.

Margarita's vigorous temperament and physical robustness stimulated the prodigious development of her feelings toward Manuel, and the situation in which destiny had placed her further stimulated the process, giving her, at the age of fourteen, the workings of a mature brain and the fruits of a twenty-year-old heart.

The two remaining alone in the room, Lucia said to her husband: "Do not think that it is only a piece of womanly wisdom, Fernando, but I believe that Margarita and Manuel love each other."

"I should be very glad to have it so, Lucia."

"But Fernando . . . the ideas of society, the duties of conscience! Margarita is the daughter of Marcela, heroic mother, victim of Don Sebastian, and Manuel is the son of the man who caused her death."

"Oh, my dear! Here is where I have the better of you," said her husband, smiling. "Manuel has let me see that there is a mystery in his birth. This history I expect to understand some day, and I can assure you that I have never believed this worthy young man is the son of Sebastian; Manuel has let slip some words at times that have entirely convinced me of the fact."

"Well, you have cheered me, Fernando; that detail will solve a problem that filled me with pain—because I have sown the seeds of aversion in the tender heart of our Margarita."

"How, in what way?"

"By indicating Manuel as the son of the man responsible for the death of her mother."

"That was very imprudent; but if she loves him, aversion will not have taken roots in her heart, and Margarita will be doubly happy the day she knows that Manuel is not the son of the abusive Governor of Killac."

"From to-day, my dear Fernando, I shall work to dissipate from the heart of my godchild the shadow which my imprudent words have cast upon it. It would really be an advantageous match for our Margarita."

"It could not be better, Lucia; I admire that young man; studious and thoughtful, he finds in his own inspirations the stimulus for work, and I foresee that he will become a distinguished lawyer, capable of adding brilliancy to the Peruvian Forum. And besides, Lucia, the means that he has at his command are more than sufficient to maintain his family well."

"Your words give me great pleasure, Fernando. They must be happy."

"It is our duty, Lucia, to try to secure the happiness of Margarita."

"I quite agree with you, Fernando. I vowed this to Marcela when she was on the threshold of her grave. She deposited in my soul the secret that Margarita is the daughter of that man, and revealed to me the particulars that you already know. And now Margarita will be as happy as I am, if she loves Manuel as I love you, my Fernando."

"Flatterer!" said Don Fernando lovingly, embracing Lucia.

Why had Lucia revealed to Don Fernando Marcela's secret? Is it true that women can never keep a secret? No! Lucia loved her husband too much to be silent, and this explains the intimacy inherent in a marriage that realises the enchanting theory of two souls blended in one, constituting thus the joy of the husband who is permitted to read as in an open book, the heart of the woman, who, in giving her hand, gives also the tenderness of a loving soul.

Marriage should not be only what it is generally believed to be, nothing but a vehicle for the propagation and maintenance of the species.

This might be the case if the senses were allowed to dominate; but there is something superior in the aspirations of the soul that seeks the source of its emanations in another soul, like the spiritual being unified by the powers of memory, understanding, and will, and bound by the holy ties of love.

Lucia, born and reared in a refined and sheltered home, when she put on her white bridal robes, accepted for herself the new home with all the charms offered by the love of husband and children, leaving to him the business and turmoil of life and following out the grand ideas of the Spanish writer, which she had read many times, seated at her mother's side. "Forget, poor women, your dreams of emancipation and liberty. Those are theories of sickly minds which can never be practised, because woman was born to grace the home."

"And now," said Don Fernando, "I must occupy myself with the family of the sexton."

"Fernando, my heart trembled with terror when Martina entered. I seemed to see the image of Marcela, and you do not know what dark presentiments filled my mind."

"Do not fear, my dear, I will not rush ahead blindly in these things, but it is impossible to allow them to assassinate another man with the stoicism of an executioner."

"I would like to be far away from Killac that I might not see nor hear of these things."

"Have patience, my dear Lucia, only a few more moments remain to you in this hateful place. Manuel will take charge of everything in conference with Guzmán; I will write to the latter now."

Going to his office, Don Fernando wrote the following letter:

Killac, December 13th, 187—
Señor Don Federico Guzmán,
Clear Water.

My dear friend:
I am on the eve of retiring to the capital, a resolution

which I have taken for reasons which you are already acquainted with.

I have need of your friendship and influence with the new Sub-Prefect to liberate from imprisonment Isidro Champi, the sexton here, who has been arrested by the true criminals in the assault of the 5th of August. I am perfectly convinced that this Indian is entirely innocent; but here nothing can be done against the machinations of the mass of the neighbours who constitute the three powers, viz. ecclesiastical, judicial, and political.

I almost dare to assure you that Estéfano Benites, Pedro Escobedo, and the Governor Pancorbo are the true culprits, the priest Pascual having left this world.

Perhaps it will seem strange to you that I should seek the intervention of the political authority in this business submitted to the justice; but if you reflect a moment upon the persons who administer justice here, you will readily understand the necessity of having some just, well-intentioned authority to compel the fulfilment of the laws. I have no interest in the prosecution of the case. My sole desire is to save the sexton whose sad fate pains me and that is all I recommend to you. If you can succeed in this I shall thank you from the very depth of my soul.

I need also a letter of recommendation from you for the Sub-Prefect in favour of Don Gaspar Sierra and family. Here they still attach a great deal of importance, my friend, to letters of recommendation, which, for me, is a good indication, because they still believe in friendship and disinterested services and have not been told that in other parts no recommendation is possible without an ounce of gold.

Give me your orders, my dear friend, and accept the kind regards of Lucia and dispose, at your pleasure, of

Your friend and servant,
FERNANDO MARIN.

Folding and sealing this letter, Don Fernando put it in his pocket and went out into the street where he expected to meet Manuel.

47

MARTINA VISITS ISIDRO

Martina penetrated into the cell where her husband was with a quick step and agitated manner, but the darkness which reigned in the place for one who entered from the light blinded her eyes for the moment. The faint light that found its way through a skylight, partly covered with adobes, at length enabled her to see the walls, the floor, and, finally, a kind of bed upon which her husband sat contemplating her without daring to ask a question for fear of hearing of some new misfortune.

On distinguishing her husband, Martina cried enthusiastically: "Isidro! Banish from your heart the black pain. Wiracocha Fernando does not prosecute us; it is false! I have seen him."

"You have seen him?"

"Yes, I have seem him, have spoken to him, and he told me that he would save you—would save us!"

"He has told you so?—and you believe it?"

"Why should I not believe him? He is not of this place, Isidro: it is only in our town that the devil shakes his cloak scattering confusion and deceit."

"And what did he ask you in payment?"

"Nothing! He did not even ask if we had sheep."

"Truly?" asked the Indian, opening his eyes.

"True, true, Isidro! And he says that it is not he who prosecutes you. I believe that he will save us, because he is sheltering the daughters of Yupanqui; do not doubt, Isidro; La Machula, Holy Mary, will be angry. The clouds do cover the sun, the evening darkens, but those clouds pass, gathered up by the one who spreads them, and the sun appears and shines and warms anew."

"Perhaps, Martinacha," said the Indian sighing and changing his position.

"By the Virgin, Isidro! Our sorrows will pass also! Without doubt you did not remember to commit yourself to the Virgin when you tolled the bells in the morning, and that is why so much misfortune has fallen upon us, like the frost that burns the leaves and blasts the ears of the corn," said Martina, seating herself by the side of Isidro.

"It may be, Martina, but . . . it is never too late to repent. The earth may be one, two, three, even four years without giving fruit. Suddenly it arouses and fills the cribs and barns."

"Well, repeat the 'Hail Mary,' and good-bye until to-morrow. I go to our children."

"What do the children say? Why do you not bring at least the little one?"

"When they ask for you, I tell them you have gone on a journey. Miguel remains silent, for he understands; I cannot deceive him longer. Bring them here? For what? It is enough that you and I should know the prison. Until to-morrow then," she said, and kissed Isidro with the chaste and peaceful kiss of a dove.

While this scene was passing between Isidro and his wife, in the house of Estéfano Benites were gathered together several neighbours commenting upon the late events over their glasses, when Escobedo arrived and called out from the door: "What have you here? Where there are so many flies there must be honey."

"Enter, friend," replied Estéfano, preparing to serve the newcomer. "Sit here"; "come this way"; "here friend," were the greetings of several.

"No, thanks, friends, I am busy," he replied, receiving the glass from Estéfano, to whom he said softly: "I need you."

"To your health, gentlemen!" said Estéfano, then retired with Escobedo to the door, where the following conversation ensued.

"Do you know that Don Fernando is taking measures in favour of Champi?"

"Ah, but do they not say that he is going away?"

"Yes. It is true that he is leaving, but that does not prevent him from defending the Indian; and if he puts in his arm we shall lose both rope and goat."

"That must not be. What! Allow ourselves to lose four— no—at least eight cows? That is not possible!"

"The son of Don Sebastian is also concerned in this matter."

"What! I do not understand what this pedantic young fellow means!"

Estéfano remained silent a few minutes with his eyes fixed on the floor. Suddenly he exclaimed: "I will hide myself with the reports and decrees."

"That is a good idea."

"What we need now is to find out on what day that brazen-faced villain Marin leaves. Of that little Manuel I have no fear. Don Sebastian is there, and, as a last resort, we will give him a beating!"

"That is it. I will ascertain immediately the day fixed for Marin's departure and the steps he is taking."

"And I will take a journey to the end of the earth. Let them find me."

"Magnificent! No sooner said than done! We shall leave that meddlesome Marin shaven and shorn."

"Let us take another drink, then let the ducks swim!" said Estéfano; both went to the table, and, after drinking the health of all present, Escobedo retired to execute his commission.

48
FERNANDO'S
PROPOSAL

Days passed on and the clouds were clearing away, leaving a brighter sky, and Manuel's financial prospects were looking brighter than he could have hoped.

Manuel was going to Lima to enter San Carlos University. His soul entertained the hope of being near Margarita, whose entrance into one of the best colleges had been resolved upon.

In the meantime, all the steps taken by Don Fernando and Manuel to have Isidro released from prison were fruitless.

The Justice shut himself up in his castle of forms and ceremonies and contented himself by offering to the parties interested a rapid despatch of the business.

Don Fernando found it impossible to postpone his journey.

He said to his wife one morning: "I have formed a plan, my dear, by which I think we can make a general reconciliation between the neighbours and ourselves, but with the idea of gaining the liberty of Isidro."

"What is it, Fernando? Oh! May God inspire you, for truly it would be very painful to go away leaving that unhappy man in prison."

"We will give a farewell banquet on the morning of our departure and there we will compromise all in favour of Isidro. I believe that they have imprisoned him only that he may appear culpable and justify themselves. Once we are gone, all motive for continuing the case will disappear, and the liberty of Isidro will be assured."

"My dear Fernando, I approve heartily of your idea and will at once order everything to be prepared, but it will cost us something, for I have seen that they try to cheat both the newly arrived and the departing guest."

"No matter, my dear; how much money is thrown away in useless things? Let it be our caprice to try to free this Indian. Will one hundred dollars be sufficient?"

"It is too much, but even if two hundred were needed, you would give it freely, I know, if it would save that poor man. Oh, the poor Indians; poor race! If we could only free all of them as we hope to save Isidro!"

As she spoke there was a knock at the door and Manuel entered with a roll of papers in his hand. Turning to Don Fernando, he said: "I come with my mind somewhat disturbed, Señor Marin. I fear that all our work has been in vain. I find that all the documents are in the hands of Estéfano Benites and he has disappeared. His wife assured me that he had gone to Saucedo and would not return for some time."

"What a bother, Manuel!"

"Perhaps he has hidden himself. That fellow has the face of Pilate!" observed Lucia.

"I do not think that, señora," said Manuel.

"The worst of it is that I cannot postpone the day of my departure if I wish to reach the train I desire to take."

"You go to-morrow?"

"To-morrow, friend; everything is ready, and to remain longer would mean delaying my journey for fifteen days. We have five days on horseback and the train comes only once in fifteen days to the Andes Station, the last on the line. But you remain, Manuel?"

"Yes, Señor Marin, I will remain and use every possible effort to accomplish our purpose."

"Perhaps by your plan, Fernando, everything can be arranged," said Lucia.

"We will see; I have thought, Manuel, to invite all the neighbours to a farewell breakfast to-morrow morning, and there speak to all in favour of Isidro, entreat them, try to obtain from them a promise to work for him."

"A very happy idea, and I think it will give good results."

"Another idea occurs to me, dear Fernando; send an invitation to Pilate, and if he is here he will surely come."

"You have re-baptised the man, Lucia," said her husband laughing.

"Not a bad idea," added Manuel, "because on his return he will see that he was included in the invitations, and perhaps he will lend us his services."

"Yes, that is right; let us see to the invitation right now, since I have no other business left; fortunately, I am free!" said Marin.

"And I will go and inspect the camp of the kitchen, because dishes prepared with forethought are the tastiest and most substantial," said Lucia, leaving the room.

"Well, Don Fernando; that idea of Doña Lucia's is a very happy one. Do you know that the invitation to Benites—or Pilate, as your wife so wittily calls him—is very important," observed Manuel.

"Ah, my friend! Women always excel us in insight and imagination. Lucia has ideas sometimes that perfectly enchant me. I assure you that each day I feel more in love with my wife. Manuel, I hope that when you marry, you will be as happy as I am."

Manuel lowered his eyes, and his face rivalled the tints of the glowing sunset sky. Margarita's name ran through his mind, wafted past in an ethereal veil of dreams, and to hide his agitation, he asked:

"How shall we phrase the invitation to Estéfano?"

"It is easy; just follow convention. Here, I will show you," said Don Fernando sitting down at the table, and after writing out several lines, he handed the paper to Manuel. This is what he read:

Residence of Estéfano Benites, 15 . . .

My esteemed friend:

Since I must leave for the capital to-morrow, and wish to take my leave, in the most cordial way possible, of the town's most notable citizens, I would like us all to take breakfast together to-morrow; and since you are one of the neighbours whom I would like to embrace before leaving Killac, perhaps forever, I most fondly hope that you will honour us with your presence.

Yours sincerely, Fernando Marin.

"That is excellent, Señor Marin, and especially the part in which we hope to shake certain hands, which we would gladly have cut off," said Manuel, folding up the piece of paper.

"Exactly! Life often imitates farce, doesn't it?"

"Well, it cannot be helped, Don Fernando. Well, then; I'll send the note with a servant."

"Thank you, my friend; and be certain to tell Don Sebastian and Doña Petronila to come."

"That I will. See you soon," said Manuel, taking up his hat and leaving.

49
THE DEPARTURE
AND
ARREST

In the yard of the White House might be seen more than twenty horses saddled; for the neighbours, on receiving the invitation of Don Fernando, wished to render him the customary honours by accompanying him a league on his journey.

Twelve mules were being loaded with the baggage which the family wished to take with them, the first part of the journey having to be made on horseback.

The guests were arriving, Manuel and his family being among the first.

The table in the spacious dining-room offered, as seasonal delicacies, fragrant strawberries and purple plums, artistically arranged in white china bowls, and enormous dishes heaped with pigeons, cooked in apple vinegar and with parsley sprigs in their beaks, as inviting to the eye as to the appetite.

The reception hall was full of people, and the Jew to whom Don Fernando had sold his house paced about with a furrowed brow, as if checking that no damage should occur to what, according to the contract, would soon be his property.

Through the chaos of animals and the moving crew that had invaded the patio stepped Margarita and Rosalia, led by a maid. They were turning their steps toward the cemetery, to pray for the last time upon their parents' grave, to shed a tear of farewell, of whose price they themselves were yet ignorant. Lucia saw to it that the orphans preserved in their hearts the relic of filial love.

Killac's cemetery was a rough, uncared-for place with here and there a rough wooden cross. But Señor Marin, solicitous, even for the grave of Juan and Marcela, had caused to be erected a cross of pure white stone to mark their resting-place. When Margarita was called on to part with her mother, she seemed like a nightingale without wings to aid her in seeking either food or nest. To-day she came to her parents' grave with her heart filled with the love of loves.

"Mother, Father! Good-bye!" murmured Margarita, after reciting "Our Father" and "Hail Mary," as Lucia had taught her.

Do girls of Rosalia's age know what it means to bid farewell forever to a mother's grave, a sacred urn that holds the ashes of the supreme love? Sorrow of sorrows! It and it alone could atone for the wanderings of a heart stripped bare of all affection!

While the orphans pay their respects, let us see what is happening in Don Fernando's house.

Just as the company was about to pass into the dining-room,

Estéfano Benites presented himself. On seeing him, Lucia, Don
Fernando, and Manuel exchanged significant glances and Lucia
gave a smile of triumph.

After saluting Lucia, Estéfano turned to Don Fernando, saying: "I only returned this morning from a little visit to Saucedo,
and, finding your letter, have come right along on the same
horse, for I wished to accompany you."

"Many thanks, Don Estéfano; that is what I expected of your
amiability," replied Don Fernando.

"Doña Petronila, kindly take the head of the table," said Don
Fernando.

"What an idea! By no means, when the priest is here!" replied
that lady.

"Yes, the priest is the one who should preside over us," was
the opinion of several.

"Very well, please yourselves. I thought of Doña Petronila on
account of the ladies."

"Yes, Don Fernando, you are right. The lady should sit here.
I will take the other side," and the priest selected a comfortable
place quite to his liking.

When all were served, Don Fernando rose to his feet, saying:
"Ladies and gentlemen, I did not wish to go away from this generous town, which has given me its hospitality, without saying
farewell to its good and noble people, and have given myself the
pleasure of gathering them together here at this modest breakfast. I drink to the health and prosperity of the inhabitants of
Killac."

"Bravo! Bravo!" was repeated in chorus.

Manuel was near Lucia, and asked her in a low voice:

"Where is your goddaughter, señora?"

"Margarita and Rosalia have gone to pay a debt of farewell;
the girls ate early. But they will be here soon."

When the repast was nearly finished, and every one was in an
excellent humour, Don Fernando, who had measured and calcu-
lated everything beforehand, rose again:

"Gentlemen. I request your attention once more. I beg my
friends to give me a proof of their affection. I wish to go away
from Killac, carrying only pleasant impressions, without leaving
any misfortunes behind me. I believe there is a prisoner in the

jail—the unfortunate sexton—and I hope that all will work for his liberation."

A great clapping of hands followed. When order was again restored, Don Sebastian said: "Let the priest speak; really, it belongs to him to answer."

"The Justice is here; let him speak," replied the priest, to which Don Hilarión responded: "For my part, I should like to have all the prisoners set free; they give me more trouble than my wife does!"

After the laughter which followed this observation had subsided, Manuel asked: "Then you give him his liberty?"

"As far as I am concerned, why not?" replied the Justice.

"Then let us drink to the freedom of my sexton," replied the priest.

"Yes, gentlemen, with full glasses," said Don Fernando; then, turning to Lucia, he added: "It is time to go."

"To your health, gentlemen!"

"A pleasant journey, Señor Marin."

"What a succulent feast! But I cannot forgive that hot chocolate; must be from Cuzco," said the priest, setting down the glass he had just drained and wiping his mouth with a napkin.

Margarita and Rosalia, who had just left a tear and a prayer on the altar of their love, returned to the Marins'. All were set to go as soon as the guests left.

Manuel took the orphan in his arms, overflowing with joy, because, with all obstacles lifted, their rose-coloured dreams, like clouds on a sunset horizon, filled those youthful hearts, heralding happy days as well for the Marins, who were eager to weave the flowery chain that would forever bind the pretty pair.

Manuel! Margarita!

May it please heaven that those ruby clouds never turn leaden or baleful.

Virtue! the golden summer sun that beautifies everything with his golden hair flowing from heaven to earth, warming and enlivening everything on the horizons of youth, making the universe smile with happiness for whomever loves and waits, had not folded his wings in Lucia's home, but struggle is inherent in life to attain perfect harmony.

Manuel and his mother had decided upon making a visit to

Lima. He would go first to arrange some business matters. He expected then to take the train to meet Don Fernando and his family, who would be waiting for him at the Grand Hotel, from whence they would continue their journey until they reached the beaches of Callao.

"Farewell, Señora Lucia!" "Good-bye, my friend!" "Margarita mine!" "Don Fernando!" "Until you return!" "Never forget Killac!" "Fortunate are those who go away!" "He who leaves forgets, and he who stays behind weeps!"

These were the words exchanged, some quickly, others with feeling.

Lucia, in her elegant riding habit, her Russian leather gloves, and her Guayaquil straw hat with a blue veil, was in the act of mounting when she let fall her beautiful ivory-handled riding whip. Don Sebastian, who stood near, made haste to pick it up and hand it to her.

At that moment there appeared at the street entrance a troop of armed men under the command of Lieutenant López, who, turning to Don Sebastian, as the troops surrounded the house, said: "By orders of the Authority, give yourself up prisoner, sir!"

If a thunderbolt had fallen in their midst, it would not have produced the effect that was caused by the words of Lieutenant López who, taking a paper from his pocket, unfolded and read it, saying: "Estéfano Benites, Pedro Escobedo, and Hilarión Verdejo will also give themselves up as prisoners!"

"Treason! Don Fernando has spread a net for us!" angrily shouted Benites.

"And, really, why do they imprison me? I should like to know," asked Don Sebastian.

Meanwhile the panic increased among those present, who could not understand the reason for these arrests; they did not remember the assault of the fifth of August, and forgot the right which belongs to a new authority to commence his period of government with acts of justice.

Don Fernando, without taking notice of Benites, called to Lieutenant López: "Sir Officer! May I know by whose order you make these arrests?"

"Certainly!" said the Lieutenant, holding out to Don Fernando the sheet which he still held in his hand. It proved to be a judicial offer given at the request of the political authority to seize the persons referred to.

Don Fernando turned to Manuel, who had approached full of anxiety. "Keep yourself calm. The worst blindfold for the eyes of reason is heat; proceed with coolness. Go and speak with Guzmán; I shall write to him by the first post."

"These are nothing but trumped-up charges!" Verdejo was saying.

"No! What do you mean, to jail?" Escobedo and Benites were shouting.

"I imagine this incident will delay your departure," said Don Fernando to Manuel, who replied, though pale as a convalescent:

"I will find a way to manage."

"I entreat you not to be so much alarmed; this will all be smoothed out in a few days; I answer for it," said Don Fernando, trying to soothe the townspeople.

"There is no reason to give up hope," said Lucia, who was also attempting to ease the general state of agitation.

"Take your horses; it is time to go!" ordered Don Fernando in a loud voice; and two groups left the house with very different destinations. One to jail, the other to the high road.

Manuel gazed upon Margarita, who was so moved that she was plunged into weeping. Her tears were the valuable pearls of a woman, with which she was sowing the unknown road on which she had set out that day, leaving behind the entire world where her cradle had been rocked and her love born.

What sorrow, to leave like Margarita!

But what greater sorrow to stay behind like Manuel, drinking drop by drop the bitterness of absence with the sighs torn from the heart by the longing of one soul crying for another!

50

COMMENTS

The scene of an arrest, in a small town, is like a conflagration in a large one.

When the soldiers left the house, taking with them their four prisoners, every doorway was filled with curious people, the small

boys marching along behind the troops, and from every side
were heard such remarks as these:

"Jesus, Mary, and Joseph!"

"Jesus protect us! Is it true?"

"What do these eyes that are returning to dust behold?"

"They say that it is an act of treachery on the part of Don Fernando; that he invited them to his house in order to have them arrested!"

"No! They say that he will be security for them."

"Security! Ha! These foreigners, they set a fire and then run away," said another.

"That's why I wouldn't eat a crust of his bread," said an old woman, looking all about her.

"Take courage, Mother, do not fear; have confidence in God," said Manuel to his mother. Giving her his arm, he conducted her home by the more retired streets.

When they arrived, she said: "Leave me, Manuel; go and do your duty."

Manuel, who had some general knowledge of law, immediately drafted a petition for his father's release, arguing that he was innocent and offering to provide the testimony of witnesses, a list of whom was attached on a separate sheet, as well as the questions that the latter should be required to answer to resolve the case.

Manuel did not close his eyes the entire night; he was consulting the Articles of Law, noting down with a pencil particular articles and composing drafts on great sheets of paper.

He opened the drawer of his writing table, and pulling out some papers, he began to go through them.

"This is the defence of Isidro Champi; shall I take it up today to defend the innocent and the guilty both at once?

"The bizarre turns life takes! This is the mysterious web of good and evil. Meanwhile, when can I leave Killac? How many months, which will seem like years, shall I be far from my Margarita?" wondered Manuel again, falling full length on the sofa, resting a few moments and returning to his work and his soliloquy.

"Above all, I must secure the release of Don Sebastian and Isidro; I will compose two separate petitions with the same purpose, asking for release on security of bail. But who could stand bail for Isidro? I need to find someone; I will tomorrow. I can be the security for Don Sebastian. . . . Now I remember, Don Fernando charged me with arranging the matter with Señor Guzmán. I will go see Guzmán, and I shall not let my body rest until this entire issue is straightened out and my soul can go fly in search of its centre. . . . Margarita! Margarita!"

The young man's invocation wafted upwards as a prayer to the God of Sleep who, beating her vapourous wings upon the law student's burning eyes, left him deep in sleep on the sofa in his room, still holding a book in his hands.

Doña Petronila wept and prayed, lifting up to heaven her concern over her husband and son; she seemed resigned to any kind of calamity, with that Christian resignation which carries one above all misfortune to the heights of heroism.

"Have faith and hope!" she said to herself, waiting for a day of calm after the horrible hours of tempest.

51
TO THE
STATION

The travellers made headway, leaving behind them the unleashed tempest.

Nature, indifferent to the painful scenes of Killac and making no effort to accommodate herself to the sadness of certain hearts, showed off her smiling and varied panoramas.

At a quick pace they crossed the seemingly interminable *pampas*, where numerous herds of cattle were grazing, climbed the hills shaded by large trees, and crept upwards around sharp rocks and on the brink of yawning chasms. During the five days' journey from Killac to the station the traveller goes crushing under his feet the wild flowers whose fragrance fills the air he breathes; then he reaches the lofty Cordillera de los Andes, where the snow, melted by the warm rays of the sun, comes

down the mountainsides in crystalline currents to the plains be-
neath, where the long grass repeats the murmuring sound of the
winds that sway it to and fro.

"Fernando, what do you think of these events which have
taken place recently?" asked Lucia in one of their intervals of rest.

"My dear, I am filled with wonder when I contemplate these
coincidences."

"God has not wished us to leave Killac without seeing the
guilty punished."

"True, dear; we should never doubt Providence, which is
sometime slow to act, but eventually does so."

"Yes, Fernando, it is true that truth will out with time and
justice with God! How will Isidro Champi fare?"

"I hope well. That Indian is innocent, of that you can be sure."

"I? I have never doubted it; I know that when the Peruvian
Indian does something wrong, he is driven by oppression, desperate from abuses."

"Look out for that gulley . . . pull the reins hard to the right,"
warned Marin.

"Whoops! If you had not warned me, I would been scared by
the jump."

"That is, if you had not fallen off first."

"I am not quite that clumsy a horsewoman. How far to the
next stop?"

"A ways still; by seven o'clock tonight we should reach our
camping-place, that is, if we make good time instead of con-
ducting a conversation."

"In that case . . . ready and . . . onward!" said Lucia, giving
her horse a smart lash.

From time to time, a horrific lightning bolt snakes its way
across these endless plains, trailing ribbons of flame, bringing
destruction to the hut, or death to the livestock, which is sent
into a frenzied stampede.

And in the midst of these imposing, solitary stretches, one
suddenly espies two reverberating steel serpents stretching along
the plains of yellow grass, and above them a cloud of vapour,
like the powerful breathing of a giant, gives life and motion to
the great cars. Suddenly the sharp whistle of a locomotive reached

their ears, shrilly announcing the progress brought by rail to the threshold where once stood the Inca Manco Capac.

"The railroad!" was the simultaneous cry of all.

It was, indeed, the train arriving at the last station in the South, located in a little village made up, for the most part, of unpainted adobe huts with thatched roofs, a woeful sight to the eye of the traveller.

A few hours after catching sight of the train, the travellers were down off their horses and heading towards a little waiting-room at the station.

There was Lucia, taking her husband's arm and lifting the long skirts of her habit with a cord hanging from her waist, the two girls in front of them, and several servants bringing up the rear.

"You go in here and tidy up; I will send the horses back, see to the luggage, and purchase our tickets," said Don Fernando, letting go of his wife's arm and pointing out the waiting-room.

"Gabino! Bring me that green valise," said Lucia to the servant who was carrying the luggage.

"Señora, shall we change our dresses?" asked Margarita, loosening the strings of her hat.

"Certainly, my dear; we will not need our riding habits anymore," replied Lucia, taking from her bag a set of keys to open the valise, and saying to her goddaughter:

"Put on your grey dress with blue ribbons. That one suits you well, and the colour is a good one for travel."

"Yes, señora, and what will you wear?" asked the orphan.

"For me, always black. For a señora there is nothing more elegant than black."

"And it looks so pretty on you."

"You flatterer! Let us see that hat."

Just then a freight train drew up, sounding "make way" with the voice of its bell. On seeing it, Gabino crossed himself, devoutly exclaiming: "Most holy Trinity . . . ! There goes the devil . . . ! Who else could move it? *Supay! Supay!*"

Don Fernando, upon his return, said, "Hurry! Señora, the train waits for no one."

"Say! Let us not be left behind!" exclaimed Lucia, packing up the floor.

"The little bottle of coca syrup? You must carry it with you,
because it is the way to ward off train sickness and the *soroche* travellers suffer at high altitudes," said Fernando, entering the room.

"There now, here is the coca," replied Lucia after she had
searched through the valise, and handed her husband a flask
carefully wrapped in pink paper with the green labels printed in
La Bolsa, in Arequipa.

"Do not forget the books either, Lucia; a train ride with
nothing to read is torture, you will see," warned Don Fernando.
Margarita then produced a package tied with brown cotton
cords and wrapped in newspaper, and handed it to Don Fernando saying:

"Godfather, here are the books; you take them, because I
need my hand free to lead my little sister."

Don Fernando took the package from the girl, tucked it under his arm, and said:

"This is important for the spirit. Gabino, take the valise."
And they all set out for the train, where the ladies of the party
were going to take their first railway journey.

52

MANUEL
FOLLOWS As burdened as Manuel was
with work, which might have
distracted him, sadness invaded his countenance and silence
sealed his lips, which had been so expressive, and now only let
out sighs of deep sorrow.

Through his heart coursed waves of blood, an unfamiliar
sensation to him; a woman's heart would have interpreted them
as omens of misfortune.

Manuel was growing apprehensive; he doubted whether he

would ever see Margarita again. Still he held firm to his resolution to straighten out the cases of Don Sebastian and Isidro, and then to leave town at whatever cost.

His interviews with the Judge handling the case, with the new Sub-Prefect, and with Señor Guzmán, finally bore fruit; one must count also the efforts made by the families of Estéfano, Verdejo, and Escobedo. One day he came home and said to Doña Petronila: "I have succeeded in getting them to take surety for Don Sebastian."

"Has the Judge decreed it?"

"Yes. Everything is arranged and at twelve o'clock we will have him at home."

"Blessed are you, child of my heart! And the others?"

"I know nothing about the others. I have tried to do something for Isidro, who will come out soon."

Doña Petronila, who had watched her son closely during these days, drew him nearer to her saying: "Apart from all these things, Manuel, there is something that makes you suffer. There is some worm gnawing at your heart that will take you to your death!" and great tears rolled down her cheeks.

"Mother, mother mine! Why do you weep?"

"Why art thou silent? My heart is the heart of a mother. Remember, Manuel, my life is thine!"

Manuel could not resist any longer. He was as weak as a woman. He had suffered so much! He threw himself into his mother's arms and hid his tears on her shoulder, just as in former years he had hidden his toys in her lap in the same manner. "Mother, mother of my soul! Blessed may you be! I feel sad unto death!" replied the youth who, timid in scenes of home and heart, could show himself a hero in the hour of combat.

"Manuel, my son, I know; I have guessed what worm gnaws at your heart—you love Margarita and weep because you are separated, and you fear you will never see her again."

"Blessed mother, forgive me if my heart is not still entirely yours; but the one whose name you have pronounced is the angel of my happiness—I love her, yes, and perhaps . . . ."

"Why do you despair, Manuel? Why can you not marry her? Why may I not have two children instead of one?"

"Mother mine, you are my Providence, but remember that Margarita will see in me the son of the man who caused the death of her parents; she will refuse my hand and cast me out of her heart." Part Two

"What nonsense! Refuse you!" replied Doña Petronila, raising her hands and remaining silent for some moments. Then, like one coming out of the excitement of battle, added: "That can be overcome easily; speak with Don Fernando and . . . reveal the name of your real father."

"Mother mine!"

"Yes, and what fault have we? It was a misfortune, and why should I not endure the shame for the sake of the happiness of my dear son, for your happiness?"

At that moment, Doña Petronila made the last sacrifice of a loving mother and of a deceived woman.

"Go," continued Doña Petronila, "overtake them on their journey; you have enough to do it with. Arrange your marriage and return happy and contented. Then you will be able to devote your entire force of mind to your family's affairs and the other journey. Right now, your mind cannot manage so much."

Manuel kissed many times the brow of his mother, her forehead, her hands; for some seconds no sound was heard but that of Manuel's lips kissing his mother, down whose cheeks rolled great tears, like the holy water that should bless the union of Manuel and Margarita.

Doña Petronila broke the silence by saying: "Enough, my dear Manuel!"

The young man lifted his head with manly pride as he replied: "To-day I swear to you, my adored mother, to sacrifice, if need be, the last breath of my life to make secure your happiness and that of my Margarita. I will go now and finish all pending matters and to-morrow at break of day will take the road and endeavour to overtake Don Fernando and ask him for the hand of his godchild."

So saying, he went out, leaving his mother absorbed in meditation.

At length, falling on her knees and covering her face with her hands, she sobbed: "Oh, merciful Virgin! I pray to thee for him who is so good and ask pardon for myself. Manuel! I! Are we culpable? Was it not the power of black fate, black as the night without morn, that conducted me to the forbidden arms of a faithless man?" Her heart shed blood, blood of her soul, remembering the scenes of twenty years before.

53
THE
JOURNEY
BY RAIL

An elegant first-class car of the machine christened with champagne as "Socabón" was ready to pull out as soon as the train whistle was heard.

Meanwhile, the first-class passengers were perusing the merchandise displayed along both sides of the track: Indian women were offering vicuña gloves, peach preserves, butter, cheeses, and fried pork rinds from the finest livestock of the mountainous interior, or *sierra,* of Perú.

Don Fernando, after seeing Lucia and the girls to their seats, made himself quite at ease beside his wife on a double seat upholstered in red plush. He took out a cigar, silently prepared it, and after lighting it put away his matchbox, let out a few mouthfuls of smoke, placed the cigar between his lips again and unwrapped the package of books; he took two further puffs on the cigar and said to his wife:

"Which would you care to read, Lucia my dear?"

"Hand me the *Poetic Works* of Salaverry," she responded with a smile of satisfaction.

"Very well, then I shall entertain myself with Palma's *Traditions;* I find these most Peruvian of tales enchanting," said Don Fernando, at the same time handing a volume to his wife.

Straightaway he stretched out and crossed his legs, propping his feet upon the frame of the facing seat, settled back, and opened his book—Palma's second collection of *Peruvian Traditions*—just as the train began to attain its running speed of fif-

teen miles an hour, swallowing up great expanses, leaving behind plains, huts, herds of grazing stock, and meadowlands at
dizzying speeds.

The various passengers sitting in their seats, whom Lucia
examined with curiosity, also began to take up their travelling
pastimes.

There was a thin military officer, a dark, bearded fellow,
seated next to two countrymen, both well along in years, veteran
traders in cochineal and sugar. The officer offered them this
invitation:

"Shall we kill time with a round of *rocambour?*"

"Fine with us, Captain, but where might we come across a
deck of cards?"

The Captain, producing a deck from his pocket, said:

"Don Prudencio, the soldier who will not gamble, drink, and
woo the ladies might just as well become a monk."

Across from them was a Brother of Mercy who, taking the
Captain's last observation personally, cast indignant glances at
the players, who, paying him not the slightest heed, turned
down the back of a neighbouring seat to equip themselves with
a card table.

The brother, for his part, drew out a book, and three women
sitting nearby struck up a conversation with Margarita and Rosalia, offering them apples peeled with a knife.

Half an hour later the girls and the women were sleeping like
doves cuddled together in the same seat, and the Brother of
Mercy was snoring, deep in the sleep of the just, not letting the
enthusiastic cries of the card-players interrupt him in his slum-
bers, until the door of the car opened and there appeared an individual of about thirty, tall, stout, with his face tanned by the
cold air of the Andes, a bushy moustache, and a fleshy mole on
his right ear.

He was wearing grey trousers and jacket; his head was covered with a cap with a black rubber visor, and he carried a ticket
punch in his hand.

"Your ticket, Reverend?" he asked, coming up to him and
raising his contralto voice, until the brother opened his sleepy
eyes and, drawing his ticket from between the pages of his book
in no great hurry, handed it wordlessly to his interlocutor.

The train conductor punched a hole in the ticket and handed it back, moving over to the site of the card game.

The two countrymen held out their respective tickets, and the Captain drew out of his inner pocket a piece of paper which he displayed to the conductor. The latter, after examining the signatures, handed it back to him, muttering to himself:

"They do everything with papers."

He came over to Don Fernando, and as he was punching their tickets, Lucia said to him:

"Would you be so good as to tell me how far we have come?"

"Four hours, Señora, that is, sixteen leagues, and we have about that much left to go," answered the conductor, and moved on.

"A marvellous journey, is it not? And without the slightest trouble, we shall soon be in the city," said Don Fernando to his wife, closing his book.

Lucía, who was looking at the girls, replied:

"Marvellous indeed, my dear! Look, Fernando, how precious they are asleep . . . ! They look like two angels of peace!"

"Of course, they are South American angels, with all the Peruvian blood that colours their cheeks."

"Could Margarita be dreaming of Manuel . . . ? She has yet to dream . . . ."

And at that very moment, her goddaughter's large eyes raised their curly lashes and fixed their gaze upon her godmother.

On that stretch of the road there rose a wooden and iron bridge, artistically placed over a shallow river.

The whistle sent out an alarm with repeated blasts, for in the very middle of the bridge was a herd of cows, whose presence went unnoticed by the engineers until they began to run in panic, but not fast enough to outpace the train.

The maneuvers of the chief engineer, the efforts of the brakemen, and the galloping of the cows were not enough to prevent a collision, and the accident was inevitable.

The "animal on wheels," huffing and puffing like a panting beast, brought first confusion and then consternation to the passengers, who were headed for almost certain death.

"Mercy!"

"God help us!"

"My husband!"

"Lucia! Girls!"

"Godmother!"

"Godfather!"

"What will become of us!"

"Beasts!"

"Mercy!"

Such were the words uttered, in various tones, amid the fright-ful confusion and shouting in the train cars.

How could they flee? They were trapped.

The entire convoy was plunging forward with the destructive speed of a lightning bolt. When it struck the cattle, it rolled right over them, shattering their bones, and leapt off the rails.

Mister Smith, the brave engineer, would rather have sacrificed his own life than those of the many existences entrusted to his keeping, and he attempted to explode the boilers by firing his revolver into them, but it was too late, and the first-class car, re-leased from its couplings by the brakeman, came to rest in the moist sand of the left bank of the river.

54
THE
PRISONERS
RELEASED

Manuel had a hundred times more work to attend to that day. He came home again, saying to his mother: "Everything is going on well. Don Sebastian is already free. The Alcalde has just passed the order, and I will go myself to conduct Don Sebastian home."

"And what conditions did the Judge impose?"

"Only that he should keep straight in all things and consider the town as his prison."

"Then we cannot go away from here?"

"You and Don Sebastian cannot, but I will go to-morrow morning, arrange with Don Fernando, and then return to your side."

"But, my son, the trial is still going to take place, and your father will have no idea how to conduct it."

"I have seen to everything for the few days I will be gone, and besides, when I come back I will have a signed statement from Don Fernando that will keep the case from going to trial," replied Manuel, pacing about.

"Or might it not be better for you to ask for Margarita's hand and those papers by mail?" said Doña Petronila, as if she regretted having agreed to let her son leave so soon.

"Mother, Mother! Under different circumstances it would be correct to write a letter, but remember I need to clarify something . . . ," observed Manuel.

"Yes, yes, I understand, but . . . ."

"Mother! A twenty-year-old heart, fiery and passionate, fears no danger, and delay is fatal to it. I am going; I will arrange my engagement and then immediately come back to your side."

"What shall I do!" she replied, shaking her head.

"Mother! Do you trust me?"

"Completely, my son; why do you ask?"

"Because I see you are hesitating; because you should understand that besides my love for Margarita, there is my duty to you and my concern over Don Sebastian, even though, when I was growing up, he treated me exactly as would a stepfather."

"Why bring that up now! He treats you well these days."

At this moment Don Sebastian entered.

"You have beaten me," said Manuel.

"Really, I expected that you would have come to bring me."

"You have come too quickly for that, Don Sebastian; I came to give my mother notice that she might not be surprised by your sudden appearance. I intended to go for you immediately."

"Very well; I am here. And now, Petronila, what have you for me to drink? Really, I am very thirsty."

"I will make you a *chabela*. There is good wine in the house, and good *chicha*."

"Now that you are at home, Don Sebastian, I will ask your blessing and permission."

"I do not understand, really."

"You are my second father. I intend to ask for the hand of

Margarita. That will cut off these discords at the root," said
Manuel with studied meaning.

"I do not disapprove of your intention, Manuel; the girl is a
pearl, but she is still a child, a little *huahua*."

"I do not think of marriage just now. I wish to ask for her,
then continue my studies and be received as a lawyer."

"That is another story, my son; really, you give me pleasure."

"He wants to go catch up with Don Fernando," said Doña
Petronila from the far end of the room, where she was mixing a
chabela on the table.

"What nonsense! Really, I tell you, Manuel, this is . . . some
kind of schoolboy stunt."

"Don Sebastian, my journey is a real necessity. My presence
here is not needed, and I must obtain a signed statement from Don
Fernando swearing he does not want charges pressed against you,
and then this entire business of the trial will be over and done
with. Otherwise, we will have legal troubles until the end of time."

"That's another matter; really, I have nothing against Manuel's
going; give him my gold watch and my vicuña wool *poncho* with
blue worked into it," replied Don Sebastian turning to Doña
Petronila, who was approaching with a glass containing an odd
mixture of liquids, yellow below and red above.

"You see, Chapaco, it's one thing to talk about your own affairs and quite another to talk about someone else's," said Doña
Petronila, handing the glass to her husband.

"Aha! Aha! Really, it's like the way a bellyache is nothing like
a toothache," said Don Sebastian, coughing and taking the glass.

"Say, there! What a cough! You must have caught cold in jail!
Poor thing!"

Don Sebastian consumed the last drop of the *chabela*, licking
his lips with a sound like a kiss, and said:

"What delicious *chabela!* Petruca, really, with this, you could
fatten up a fasting hermit." And then he asked Manuel: "How
and when are you going?"

"Early tomorrow, sir."

"Good. So give him everything he needs, Petruca, and let him
pick the best horses and all that, since, really, when we're far from
home people treat us according to the impression we make."

"Thank you, sir! So many favours!" replied Manuel, and went out to prepare for the journey.

It was nine o'clock that night when Manuel came back and went into Doña Petronila's room; there he found Don Sebastian in an obviously quite private conversation with his mother.

"Good evening, Don Sebastian. Mother mine, I have come to take my leave; all is completely arranged, thanks to the help of God," said Manuel.

"My son! May the Virgin bear you along with life and health and return my son to me," answered Doña Petronila, taking a scapulary of the Virgin of Carmel that she wore around her neck and placing it on Manuel's chest, then embracing him tenderly.

"Don Sebastian, be as prudent and discreet as possible ... keep your own counsel and silence, silence! No one will give you any trouble. You should not worry about me. A hug and farewell!"

"Don't be long, don't be long . . . . Really, your journey fills me with hope . . . . Did you take the watch?" said Don Sebastian, taking his leave of Manuel, who went off to rest in his room, since with the first glimmer of daybreak, borne on the wings of hope and with the energy of the young, he would set out on the same route that only days before he had seen his enchanting Margarita take.

Isidro Champi, accompanied by his faithful Martina, arrived at his house that day, pale and sad.

As he came in, his children came running to him as a flock of partridges to their mother. The heart of the sexton, which was dark as the cave of a witch, received light and warmth from the kisses of his children as he caressed them in silence. Martina entered the cabin slowly and knelt down in the middle of the room, lifting her clasped hands to heaven. "*Allpa* mamma!" she exclaimed, smothering in her breast all the burdens that her wounded soul could have laid bare to the unjust humanity represented by the town notables of Killac, and her eyes shed copious tears.

"Still crying, Martina? Has the rain of your heart not yet ceased?" asked Isidro, noticing his wife.

"Alas, my husband!" replied Martina rising. "Pain swims in tears as the gull plunges into the waters of the lake, and, like her, wets her feathers but refreshes her breast, alas!"

Isidro seemed consoled by the presence of his children; but on looking them over, calling them by their names, thoughts of his lost heifers came to his mind and he murmured, sighing: "The chestnut, the black!"

"Ah, Isidro, in the stormy night when the lightning flashes and the thunder peals among the rocks, man shelters himself in his cabin and the foxes and the pumas leave their dens to rob and slay the lambs. For us has raged the fierce tempest," said Martina, seating herself on the rough bed by the side of the youngest child.

"For the puma and fox we have the trap of the yellow stone; but from our oppressors there is no way of freeing ourselves."

"Patience! patience! Isidro, death is sweet to the sad," added the wife.

"The brave must be tranquil as the moon-lit night in which the shepherd's song makes sweet music! Ah! If we did not have these chicks, how sweet it would be to die!" said Isidro, pointing to the children who were shouting and leaping around the eldest boy.

Martina replied: "We were born slaves of the priests, slaves of the Governor, slaves of the *cacique*; slaves of everyone who holds the rod of authority."

Isidro doubled his *poncho* and put it under his head for a pillow saying: "Indians! Yes. Death is our sweet hope of liberty."

Martina came to his side, wishing to turn his thoughts from his dark sorrow, and said, passing her hand through his hair: "Will you go up to the tower again?"

"Perhaps," replied the Indian. "To-morrow I shall have to ring those cursed bells which from to-day I hate."

55

A TERRIBLE SHOCK

The first to leap to the ground, landing in mud up to his knees, was Mister Smith, and he shouted at the top of his lungs:

"Hey! Nobody move! Everybody stay quiet!"

Just then a multitude of heads peered out the car's windows, not one pane of which remained intact.

The crash that threw the first-class car off the tracks fortunately had caused only minor injuries.

"What a blood-chilling experience! My dear, was it much of a shock for you?" said Don Fernando of Lucia.

"Oh yes, my dear. God alone has saved us!"

"You look very pale. Has the bottle of coca been broken?" asked Marin, searching in a small carrying case.

"My God . . . !" Lucia exclaimed again, peering out the train window to see where they were, and not noticing the screams of Margarita, who was raising up Rosalia, covered with blood, or what the other passengers were saying.

"Just think what might have happened to us!" said the military man.

"We have been born again! Blessed be God!" said the monk.

"These stupid *gringos* could take us down to hell!" said one of the card-players, to which another added:

"I was afraid of something like this ever since I saw the reverend come aboard."

"Hush . . . ! There are ladies present!" said the individual in question.

"How did we come out of all this?"

"Well, the coca syrup was saved; I shall give you a little, my dear," said Fernando, looking in his pocket for a little knife with a corkscrew.

"Luckily, the car had already passed over the bridge by the time it derailed, so no great damage was done," said a brakeman, running from one side of the car to the other, stringing cords. Several different people asked him:

"My good man, what do we do now?"

"Nothing, sir, it is nothing; everything is over," replied the brakeman.

While this was happening in the first-class car, the passengers in the second-class car, which had quick-wittedly been uncoupled and remained undamaged at the far end of the bridge, were running toward the first car, run aground, and shouting:

"Paulino!"

"Indalecio!"

"Over here, man!"

"The devil!"

"Calm yourself, señora; it is not my fault, can you understand that? The cows are to blame, and everything can be soon set to rights," said Engineer Smith, embellishing the Spanish tongue like a good son of North America; his speech instilled confidence in the troubled spirits of the first-class passengers.

"Mister Smith, when can we expect to arrive? This was nearly the end of us!" said Don Fernando, turning to the engineer, whom he knew.

"Oh, Señor Marin, what fate has brought me! But the train will arrive to-morrow, have patience," replied Mister Smith, supervising the repairs.

And with the energy that typifies the North American race, winches, cables, and pulleys were set into motion, so that, after two hours of ceaseless labour, they pulled out the car that had run aground in the sand and placed it back on the rails, ready to continue the journey.

"Truly, we have been born again; my poor daughters!" said Lucia, wiping away with her handkerchief the blood that was coming out of Rosalia's lips from an injury to her mouth.

"Oh, my Lord! Hush, my child . . . ! Poor girl . . . !" added Don Fernando, approaching the little girl with a package of sweet biscuits, which he placed in her hands.

"It will be another five hours yet," said the artillery captain.

"These things happen only in Perú; anywhere else, they would have had the *gringo*'s hide," observed the cochineal trader.

"My soul has still not quite come back to my body."

"Nor has mine, good gracious!" said the two women.

And the train resumed its swift, steady journey, just as before that catastrophe.

The whistle was heard again and again, insistently.

"Another accident?" asked several startled passengers.

"No, this is the second station before we come to the city; the whistle is the signal of our arrival."

"Heavens! A scare like that leaves one's entire body nervous," observed Lucia.

"It was a serious matter," answered Don Fernando.

Presently the travellers were pointing out, through the broken window panes, a white spot in the midst of a great sweep of lively, merry green.

"The city!" several exclaimed.

And the whistle sounded again, like an animal impaled by a piercing weapon.

"What beautiful countryside! What a lovely city!" said Lucia, stretching her head farther out the window.

"It looks like a white dove in its nest among the willows," added Señor Marin. His wife asked him:

"Fernando, is it the second city in Perú? What are its people like?"

"Yes, my dear, the second. The beauty of the city can only be compared to the kindness of its daughters. You will enjoy our stay greatly," replied her husband.

And the station bell gave word that the convoy was entering the main depot of the city, where a large crowd was waiting, for news of the accident had been spread by telegraph, and curiosity had drawn hundreds of people.

When the cars were opened, hordes of porters rushed up to the travellers and demanded to carry their luggage. Fernando Marin and his family were transformed from railway travellers to riders of flesh-and-blood transportation, which took them to the very door of the Grand Imperial Hotel, where they clambered down.

56
GRAND
IMPERIAL
HOTEL

They went into a spacious salon, with wallpaper of an oxblood colour trimmed with gold, and great square golden columns; the doors and windows, covered with draperies of an

ermine whiteness, crowned with a flourish of red damask with
gold edging, and tied back with silken cords. The floor, covered
with rich Brussels carpets, made a pleasant contrast with the
Louis XV furniture, upholstered in opaque blue silk, and multi-
plied by two enormous mirrors that covered the right wall almost in its entirety.

"This is the reception room. Does the señora find it to her
liking?" said Monsieur Petit, bending over with exaggerated
deference.

"Yes, blue is my favourite colour; I shall be happy here," said
Lucia to the hotelier, Monsieur Petit.

"This must be a bedroom?" asked Don Fernando, indicating
a door that opened off the salon.

"Exactly, señor; here are all the comforts and full service at
the disposition of the travellers who honour with their presence
the Grand Imperial Hotel," answered Monsieur Petit with all the
suavity of a Frenchman, praising his own establishment.

"So we would hope."

"If you should need anything, my señor, my señorita, this
cord rings the service bell," said the hotelier, making his departure with a bow.

Margarita, who was examining everything she saw with the
most minute attention, asked with candid simplicity:

"Señora, what would Manuel say if he saw this?"

Lucia smiled to herself the smile of a mother enjoying the ardour of youthful feelings, reading in that question the entire
poem of a virginal heart's memories, and she answered:

"He can tell you himself when he comes."

"Are we awaiting his arrival?"

"Why, yes, my child," Don Fernando assured her, entering
into the intimate exchange between godmother and goddaughter.

Rosalia went over and embraced Señor Marin about the knees,
saying:

"Give me another biscuit."

The servant appeared in the door, leading in the boy with the
luggage.

A week was sufficient for the travellers to become acquainted
with the populous city, observing everything and searching out

its tendencies and customs, with the thoroughness of the traveller who already brings a rudimentary knowledge that will develop before the open book of learning acquired in the practical school of the great wide world.

Streets wide and straight but badly paved; Moorish-style temples, browned and stained by the passing years; women, beautiful as a golden legend; robust countrywomen with all the candour of their souls depicted in their countenances; pawnshops with buying and selling prices posted; theatres; business houses of all classes and grades—nothing escaped the minute observation of Lucia, aided and facilitated by the knowledge and observations of Don Fernando, to whom one day she said:

"I declare to you, Fernando, this would be a celestial mansion were it not for the moral inconveniences that I have noted in my simple experience."

"I know them, my dear; I knew them beforehand, the reluctance of the soul to remain in one place, the anxiety to arrive in Lima, the centre of light that captures all the butterflies of Perú."

"I like your logic, Fernando, but you have failed to find the key," replied Lucia, laughing and giving him a pat on the shoulder.

"No . . . ? Well, tell me, then, what has most struck you here?"

"There are two things that I have noticed particularly," said Lucia levelly, using her handkerchief to pat her lips, slightly moist from her laughter.

"Ah . . . ! I know! You are playing games!" said Don Fernando, returning the affectionate pat.

"Tell me then, what are they? You won't guess."

"I know one of them is the number of friars of all colours who go about the streets."

"You went straight to Rome, my dear."

"So . . . what might the other be?"

Lucia became grave; her spirit seemed to be considering something far away. Breathing a sigh which seemed to come from the depths of her heart, she said: "What has most attracted my attention is the surprising number of orphans in the orphan asylum here. Ah, my Fernando! I know that the countrywoman does not cast away in that manner the pieces of her heart.

She has no need to throw them away, because in her case those
social considerations which put on the mask of feigned virtue
do not come between the mother and the child that came by
chance or by crime! Fernando, may God pardon my wrong
thought, remembering without wishing to do so the secret of
Marcela."

Don Fernando listened with surprise to Lucia, realising that
she was reasoning out a problem in moral philosophy. He was
overpowered by the brightness of a great soul of whose superiority he was, perhaps, ignorant until that moment. Silence
reigned for a moment, then he sighed with perhaps as deep a
pain as Lucia's, saying:

"Poverty, also, sometimes opens the doors of the asylum."
Then approaching her, he impressed a kiss on the brow of she
who would soon be the mother of his first-born.

57
THE
AGATE
CROSS

Manuel had a pleasant journey in every respect. It was as if
the winged gods of Love and Marriage had cast their amber
breath over the snowy wastes and fields of wild grass that the
trailway traversed; Manuel knew nothing of the danger that
days before had menaced the Marin family and, with it, his
Margarita, that poem of tenderness that for him was intoned
with notes drawn from the most delicate fibres of his heart, like
the Aeolian harp, set to resounding by the fluttering of the
vapourous wings of the Angels of Happiness soaring above the
immense plains.

He also made out on the horizon the city of his dreams. At
that moment, this low-lying Andean city was, in his mind, the
sultan of the world, because it was hosting the queen of his
heart. He arrived; he went to take lodging in the Hotel Casino

Rosado. Waiting only to shake off the dust of travel and array himself in suitable attire, Manuel turned his face towards the Imperial Hotel, saying to himself:

"Thanks to you, my God! I shall see her! How true it is that at twenty the blood burns and any delay is exasperating! I cannot set back even one more day the realisation of my happiness . . . but . . . I will speak right away with Don Fernando . . . . There is the need for prudence, to keep a firm rein on the soul's urges. Already, during the days of her absence, jealousy has begun to prickle me with its poisoned needle . . . . Oh! How can I but think that Margarita's Peruvian beauty, the loveliness of her soul, still virgin to the world's self-seeking phrases, will attract a flock of suitors, who will ply her ears with words that will stain the heart of the woman I love . . . ?"

Manuel walked along like one drunk, noticing nothing in the streets through which he passed for the first time, obeying mechanically the directions given him by the doorman at the Casino Rosado.

"Jealousy is ruinous, but at the same time it is noble," he resumed his interior musings. "In the depths of the most supreme and satisfied love jealousy dwells, curled up like a viper; in the case of a common love, the serpent writhes and slithers across to sink in its poisoned fangs. May my jealousy never awaken! My love for Margarita is great indeed . . . !"

Manuel's footsteps resounded in the patio of the Imperial Hotel, and the sound sent shivers through Margarita's soul.

Why does the woman in love recognise not only the footsteps of her beloved, but even the perfume of his breath at a distance and the echo of his voice, which for her has a special vibration amidst a multitude of other voices?

Mysteries of the magnetic current that unites two souls, shaking the organism to its core!

The glass door swung on its hinges; the wind lightly stirred the fine draperies, and Manuel appeared in the blue room, with the most distinguished and engaging bearing.

Margarita, standing by a little table on which was a Chinese vase filled with jasmine and daffodils, filling the room with their fragrance, whispered to herself, "It is he!"

"Señora! Señor!" he said, extending his hand to each in turn, who returned his salutations cordially.

"Margarita mine . . . !"

"Manuel! You have come!"

The two young people were about to embrace, but some force held them back. Nonetheless, their eyes translated the embrace of two souls dreaming of becoming one forever.

"Sit down and tell me all the news from Killac," said Don Fernando.

"People there are well, sir."

"Was your father's problem resolved? Was the poor sexton, Isidro, released from jail?"

"Don Sebastian has come out free without much trouble, but as for Isidro, I have been required to file a number of petitions and statements to obtain his release. So I come with a happy heart after having carried out the mission with which you entrusted me, Don Fernando."

"My good man! You are a true gentleman. I was unable to send you the letter for Guzmán; there was not a single postal drop to be found along the entire route. And the political authority . . . is still . . . ."

"Bad, very bad, Don Fernando. The first few days, it seemed as if the new broom would sweep clean. Later, as I found out, he took some yearling cows in exchange for the freedom of Estéfano, Escobedo, and Verdejo."

"It is clear to see, my friend, that the situation is hopeless," said Don Fernando, rising from his seat.

"And how did you like my guesswork concerning the journey Estéfano claimed to be taking?" Lucia asked Manuel.

"Ah! Señora! You ladies will always outdo us in dealing with malice, and you are the best judges of human character. I have grown to detest that individual," replied Manuel.

"Those pettifoggers, half-educated and blindly ambitious, are the ruination of those poor towns," said Don Fernando.

"They are . . . Pilates, as the señora called them," added Manuel with a smile.

"Gracious! This is the first day I have laughed since that scare," observed Lucia, looking at Margarita, who was also smiling.

"You are aware of the near tragedy in which we were involved during the train journey?" Don Fernando asked Manuel.

"No, señor; what happened?"

"Well, we just barely escaped being killed and crushed in a train wreck."

"How was that?" asked Manuel; a shiver coursed through him and he looked at Margarita.

"The train left the tracks. You heard nothing about it on your way to Lima?"

"Yes, now I remember something, I heard two passengers discussing it, but I thought they were speaking of something that happened a long time ago."

"Gracious, what dreadful scenes we saw!" interrupted Lucia.

"Rosalia was injured," said Margarita.

"And the two of you?"

"There was no further damage, fortunately, and it was all attended to. Let us not speak further of the accident; it will be bad for Lucia's nerves," said Don Fernando.

"Now that is a real matter, Señor Marin."

"What were you saying the Judge required before he would free Isidro?" asked Don Fernando.

"For the case to be resolved definitively, I need to obtain from you a statement in which you swear that the attack on your house was simply the result of an error, the attackers believed themselves to be pursuing some robbers whom they thought had taken refuge in your house, and it was nothing but an excited crowd, and so forth. And then I will return immediately to arrange everything, to make certain that Don Sebastian is not troubled further, and to prepare to leave for Lima again, this time to stay."

"I will compose a clear statement that will lay the matter to rest, my friend. I will never return to Killac, and I want to ensure the safety of that poor Indian; someone might still want to stir up trouble for him. Do you think a signed statement from me will put an end to this entire business?" asked Señor Marin.

"Yes, Don Fernando; without that document, the authorities could still take action in the case."

"So you have freed Isidro Champi. Oh! Who will free his entire disinherited race?"

"That is a question that should be asked of all Peruvians, my dear friend . . . !"

"So you are returning to Killac?" asked Lucia.

"Yes, señora."

"And will we not stay on together in Lima?" said Margarita, twisting a jasmine that she had pulled from a bouquet.

"Yes, Margarita, I will and go and return; travel is simple for a man," answered Manuel.

"And Doña Petronila, how is she?" asked Lucia.

"You can imagine, señora, how the poor woman is doing with me far away!"

"Well, then, the mail goes out tomorrow; so I shall prepare the statement to Guzmán immediately, and it will arrive before you; now I have to go out and attend to some business; forgive me," said Don Fernando, rising to his feet.

"Fine, Señor Marin; it will save time to send the document to Señor Guzmán; but . . . I have some very important business about which I wish to consult you; when will you be at liberty to attend to me?" asked Manuel, visibly in the grip of emotion, as he took up his hat.

"To-night, my friend. After eight o'clock I shall be at your service."

"Come and take chocolate with us," invited Lucia.

"Thank you, señora; I shall not fail to come," answered the young man, politely taking his leave, and behind him swung shut the glass-panelled door that separated him from the empress of his existence.

Back outside, he began to roam the streets of the city, and as he was passing by a jeweller's shop, he saw a beautiful agate cross, delicately framed in a gold setting and lying in its purple velvet box.

"What a beautiful piece! How lovely it would look on Margarita's bosom," thought Manuel, and he stopped to examine it more closely. "I shall buy it!" he resolved. Entering the shop, he purchased it with three thick bank notes, and transferring the jewel to his pocket, he continued on his way, absorbed in the thoughts that were fluttering about in his mind, some like glowing filaments, and others like swallows that, in passing flight, brush by lightly with their black wings.

58
BIRDS
WITHOUT
A NEST

The moon, which only hours earlier had begun to wane, suspended in a cloudless sky, shed its silvery light, which, even if it provides no heat, does not wound the eyes like the sun's rays. Its glow imbues nature with a sweet, serene melancholy, and offers a warm, fragrant atmosphere on those December nights created for colloquies of love.

Manuel, restless and moody, consulted his gold watch at frequent intervals.

The hands signalled the appointed hour, and, taking up his hat, he left at a good pace.

The glass-panelled doors to the blue room of the Imperial Hotel, which was brilliant with the light of elegant crystal chandeliers, stood wide open to receive him.

Margarita was seated by the table and the flowers, playing with the border edging of a white handkerchief, with her mind transported to the heaven of her dreams, and the deepest hush reigning about her.

When Manuel appeared in the doorway, she nimbly changed positions, and her eyes turned towards the bedroom door, where, no doubt, Lucia was to be found.

"Margarita, soul of my soul! I came, I have come for you!" said Manuel, taking the girl's hand and sitting down beside her.

"Truly? But here you are going away," she replied without drawing away her hand, which was gently squeezing Manuel's.

"Have no doubt of my devotion, my dear Margarita; I have come to ask you of Don Fernando for my wife!"

"And Doña Lucia, will she know?" interrupted the girl.

"I shall ask both of them . . . you shall be mine," said the young man, gazing deep into Margarita's eyes as he drew her hand to his lips.

"And if they are not willing?" asked Margarita innocently, blushing and casting her eyes to the floor.

"But you do love me . . . . Margarita! You love me, do you not? Answer me, for the love of God!" Manuel insisted, overcome by an anxiety that was evident in his gaze, which consumed everything upon which it lit.

"Yes," timidly replied Marcela's daughter, and Manuel, dizzied by his good fortune, brought his lips towards those of his beloved; he breathed in her breath, and drank the purest drop of dew from souls in the chalice of joy; the drop only left him with a greater thirst.

Margarita, deeply stirred, said only:

"Manuel!"

With the timeliness of events in a novel, Manuel at that exact moment remembered something important; he put his hand into his pocket, brought forth the little velvet case, opened it, and presenting her with the jewel, said:

"Margarita, on this cross, I swear to you that my first kiss of love shall never stain your honour . . . ! Keep it for my sake, my dear; agate has the power to strengthen the heart!"

Margarita took the cross almost mechanically, closed the little box, and hid it in her bosom as if it were stolen goods, as just then the glass-panelled doors to the bedroom groaned on their hinges and Lucia and Don Fernando emerged.

Manuel could scarcely keep his emotions in check.

His countenance was the colour of pomegranate flowers, and a slight tremor seized his entire organism. Should we have been able to reach out and take his hand, we would have found it moist with cold sweat; penetrating into his brain, we would have seen a hundred ideas swarming about like bees, fighting to be the first to burst out in the form of words.

Margarita, who was stunned by the new sensations coursing through her heart, could hardly disguise her state of mind.

"Something serious has happened to you, Manuel," said Don Fernando, looking intently at the young man.

"Señor Marin," he replied in a trembling voice, scarcely able to complete his sentence, "it is . . . the most serious thing I expect . . . in my life . . . ! I love Margarita and I have come . . . to ask for her hand . . . following . . . a three-year . . . engagement."

"Manuel, I should be greatly pleased, but . . . Don Sebastian?"

"Señor, I know your argument, and it is necessary that I

begin by destroying it. I am not the son of Don Sebastian Pancorbo. A misfortune, the abuse of a man on the weakness of my mother, gave me my being. I am linked to Don Sebastian by gratitude, because, on marrying my mother, he gave her the honour, and to me . . . he lent his name."

"Thank God!" exclaimed Margarita, raising her hands in praise to heaven, unable to keep silent.

"My dear child," murmured Lucia.

"Your nobility obliges us to make use of the right that Marcela, before her death, gave to us when she confided her secret to Lucia," replied Don Fernando gravely.

"I am glad, Don Fernando; the child is not responsible in these cases, and we must always cast the blame on the laws of men and never upon God."

"That is so."

Manuel lowered his voice, and with a look of shame, said: "Don Fernando, my father was Don Pedro Miranda y Claro, former priest of Killac!"

Don Fernando and Lucia both turned pale as if struck by an electrical current; surprise tied a tight knot in both their throats, and absolute silence reigned for some moments, a silence that was broken only with Lucia's exclamation:

"My God . . . !" And she clasped and wrung her hands until the joints creaked.

There passed through the mind of Don Fernando like a flash the name and life of the priest Pascual, and he said to himself, "Will the wrong-doing of the father cut off the happiness of two angels of goodness?" And, as if doubting the truth of what he had heard, he asked again: "Whom did you say?"

Manuel, appearing less agitated, answered quickly:

"Bishop Claro, señor."

Don Fernando approached Manuel and, embracing him, answered: "You yourself have said it, Manuel. We cannot blame God, but we must blame the inhuman laws of man that take the father from his child, the nest from the bird, the stalk from the flower!"

"Manuel! Margarita . . . ! Birds without a nest . . . !" interrupted Lucia, white as the almond flower, unable to contain her grief, and great tears rolled down her cheeks.

Manuel could not explain to himself the meaning of that scene, while Margarita was mute, trembling like a lily stricken down by the tempest.

The word of Don Fernando must come to put an end to that agonising situation, but his manly voice, always firm and frank, trembled like that of a boy. Sweat broke out on his noble, raised brow, and he shook his head; at moments he seemed to express doubt, at others astonishment.

At last, indicating Margarita, as if commending her to the care of his wife, he turned to Manuel, saying:

"There are things in this life which overwhelm us . . . ! Have courage, young man . . . unfortunate young man . . . ! Marcela, on the borders of the grave, confided to Lucia the secret of the birth of Margarita, who is not the daughter of Juan Yupanqui the Indian, but of . . . Bishop Claro!"

"My sister!" "My brother!" exclaimed with a single voice Manuel and Margarita, the latter falling into the arms of Lucia, whose sobs accompanied the sorrow of those tender

BIRDS WITHOUT A NEST.